MAX:
IT SHOULD
ONLY BE

MAX:
IT SHOULD
ONLY BE

by
PETER
BERCZELLER

Published by Repeater Books
An imprint of Watkins Media Ltd
19-21 Cecil Court
London
WC2N 4EZ
UK

www.repeaterbooks.com

A Repeater Books paperback original 2017
1

Distributed in the United States by Random House, Inc., New York.

Cover design: Johnny Bull
Typography and typesetting: Josse Pickard
Typefaces: Sabon/Requiem

ISBN: 978-1-910924-55-6
Ebook ISBN: 978-1-910924-67-9

This book is dedicated to every single member of my family.
In the words of those ubiquitous handbills circulated in the
Old West: They are wanted, dead or alive.

Memory is history censored by the brain.

— Franz von Loewensberg
(Minor 19th-century German philosopher)

PART ONE

CHAPTER ONE
REVENGE FANTASIES

June 1984

I'm not a gutsy guy. Never have been. Giving – or even getting – a bloody nose has no place in my repertoire. The only time I ever use a knife is when there's a brain to be carved up. The same goes for killing people. Which, for us doctors, is a big no-no. Our job is to keep patients on top of this earth, not six feet under. In medical school, we'd have those endless, middle-of-the-night discussions on what we'd do if Hitler were brought into the ER. In Argentina, presumably, in 1945, bleeding to death from bullet holes tracing out a Star of David on his chest. Give him blood transfusions, put a tube into his trachea, run him to the OR? Or drag it out, wasting a minute for each million he killed, concentrating on the calligraphy of the "Do Not Resuscitate" order prematurely placed on his gurney?

I've always been for the first option. Playing God is never an alternative, where you're the one to decide who's to live and who's to go down the drain. I'd bust my ass to treat patient Adolf; that's the doctor part of me talking. But then, once he's better, I'd wish him the worst. When I'm off duty, I'm not hindered by the scruples I was just bending your ear about. Taking the law into your own hands does make a lot of sense in very special circumstances. For instance, a guy comes home from work early. As soon as he opens the door, he hears a loud moaning coming from the bedroom. He charges in, and catches his wife in *flagrante delicto*, the ecstatic look on her face explaining the unfamiliar sound coming through the door. The perfect setup for a crime of passion. Not that I'm advocating vigilante justice, but the toxic mix of adrenaline and testosterone urging the finger to pull the trigger, or the hand to plunge the knife, may just be impossible to resist.

That's what's called acute revenge. No lag time between the deed and the response. It's high drama for all the participants: the cuckolded husband, the wife whose voice instantly changes register from moans to groans, and of course the soon-to-be-dead – or at the very least maimed – unwelcome visitor.

Nothing like what's been building up in me all these years. The need to whack my real father's executioners simmering on a low flame, with very little hope for ever coming through with the real McCoy. A classic case of if I could I would, but I can't, so I won't.

A while ago, my research led me to a special spot in the brain. Jiggle it the right way, and it'll do something to surprise you. I call it the "suicide center." For good reason. Nudge it into doing its specialty act, and, next thing you know, you've got a suicide on your hands. So far, it's worked fine with laboratory animals. Now I'm about to try it on humans. The pipe dream I've had since I was a kid found a new home when I had this "Dr Livingstone, I presume?" moment. That's the reason I'm on my way to Austria right now.

Five of the seven (the other two died during the war) who assassinated my father, are still around. Four of them in St Marton, a small Austrian town on the Hungarian border, and one, Weissensteiner, in nearby Wiener Neustadt. Franzl – that's what the good old boys who frequented his tavern called him – was the honcho in charge of the killers, automatically putting him at the very top of my hit list. You know how parents bring up the Boogie Man when they want to scare the shit out of their children? For me, it was the name Weissensteiner that did the trick. I kept on hearing that word, that name, when my folks shifted to German so I couldn't follow what they were talking about. Looking somber and frightened while they were talking gibberish in front of me. It didn't take long for Weissensteiner to become my own special Boogie Man.

Every night, he'd rise up at the foot of my bed like a genie. The blue eyes and harsh look of Tommy Byrnes, our neighborhood bully, merging with the closest resemblance to the devil I could think of: the Joker, from the Batman comics. He'd come all the way to Fort Lee, New Jersey, to spirit the three of us back to St Marton. Meanwhile slitting the throat of our dog Hugo and setting the house on fire. By then I was in panic mode, holding onto my little prick like a drowning dog grabbing at a branch. After a while, Phase 2 would kick in. Relief. I was in my bed, and the dog was snoring next to me. I'd held off Weissensteiner for another night.

I never found out my family's real story until I was almost sixteen. According to the earlier, bogus version, my parents got married right after my father finished dental school. They settled down in St Marton, but, a few years later, the Germans marched into Austria. Out of nowhere, swastikas everywhere. Weissensteiner was the boss of the Nazi operation in the town. Under him were Strobl, the game warden; Baumgartner, the owner of the local sawmill; Kleinert, the head of the Gendarmerie; Wagner, the jailkeeper; Hochberger, the butcher on the main square; and Czemenecz, the school principal and Weissensteiner's brother-in-law. Between them they made life miserable for the Jews. Walked into their houses and helped themselves to whatever caught the eye. Furniture, pictures, silverware, cash, you name it. From the get-go, they arrested Erich, my father, and Doctor Brenner, my parents' best friend, who was their next door neighbor. Also Feivel, the Rabbi's oldest son, Wurmfeld the lawyer, and a couple of the more prosperous businessmen of the *Judengasse*, the ancient ghetto. They put them all in the local jail. The beatings, courtesy of Weissensteiner and crew, began right away. They pulled Feivel's *pejes*, his forelocks, out with pliers. Knocked out teeth, broke some ribs. Brenner was their special target. Not only was he a Jew, but, even worse in their eyes, a socialist. They took him out to the courtyard that night, and told him he was about to be shot. Put him up against the wall, and cocked their guns. At the last minute, they backed off. "Just kidding," they yelled, as if it was all a big practical joke.

After several days, the Nazis released the prisoners. A couple of weeks after, there were no Jews left in town. A convoy of open trucks took them, and their two suitcases per family, to Vienna. A week later, the Judengasse and the four-hundred-year-old temple were dynamited.

When I was around sixteen, a letter came in the mail. It bore foreign stamps, and the return address was intriguing. From what I could understand, the sender was a committee for victims of Fascism. The name of the recipient on the envelope was "Frau Brenner." The only Brenner I'd ever heard of was their friend in St Marton, the one who was put against the jailhouse wall for the fake execution. I couldn't figure it out.

I got my answer that evening when I asked why my mother was called Brenner. She couldn't stop sobbing, while Erich kept pacing up and down, hands clenched behind his back. It turned out my mother was originally married to Dr Richard Brenner. He was my father, not Erich, who was their bachelor best friend across the hall. She was a couple of months pregnant with me when Richard and Erich were arrested. Richard must have known that Weissensteiner and his boys weren't going to be satisfied with batting him around like the other Jews. That's why, early on during their first night in jail, he asked Erich to watch over his wife and unborn child if anything happened to him. His premonition was on the button. After beating up the others, they came for Richard last. The large cell where the prisoners were held looked out on the jail courtyard, so they had a direct view of what happened next. My father – my real father – was stood up against the wall. No fake execution in this up-to-date version of the events. Real bullets were fired from each of the seven hunting rifles on the firing squad. After the shooting, they all clapped each other on the back and went back inside, leaving the body – it was still twitching – where it had fallen.

Until that day, revenge against the people who drove my parents away from their homeland was not something I'd ever thought about. No reason to feel bad about Richard Brenner. Hadn't he lived to tell the tale after being stood up against the wall? I'd even made up a story about the ones who stayed behind. Onkel Adolf, Tante Cecilia and their children, Arpad and Paul, whose pictures, old-time posed studio prints, stood on top of the piano. Seeing them there ever since I could remember, I felt like I knew them. I'd even turn their pictures one way or another, hoping for some magical sign from their eyes that they knew I missed them, even though we'd never met. The truth – that they were deported and killed – must have been too terrifying for me to absorb. In my fictional version, they got away at the last minute, ending up in a safe place. Palestine was in the news a lot at that time–maybe there?

A child who's born with only one parent left alive is in a special bind. To actually be touched and held by your father or mother, and afterwards hear the song and dance about mommy or daddy having gone to heaven, is a special calamity. You spend part of the rest of your own life looking for them in every little corner, increasingly convinced the business about heaven was just a fanciful rumor. And tough as that is, it's even worse when you find out your parent has been murdered. That it could have been avoided, it didn't need to happen. Somebody–not some sickness or accident–was to blame for the void in your life.

Finding out about my real father was not the only revelation to hit me that evening, when the real story behind the myth my parents had cooked up finally emerged. I became so tied up–had to be–with my shock at finding out that the man who I thought was my father all along was just a last-minute pinch hitter. Erich did the right thing. Married his best friend's widow–no way of ever knowing if she was really his cup of tea–and raised their child as his own. Ever since I could remember, I'd never had any reason to suspect Erich wasn't my real father. I was so preoccupied with Richard–not only how he died but also how he lived–that everything Erich had ever done for me as I was growing up now seemed the work of an impostor. While he was still alive, I never spoke to him about this struggle within myself. It ended up as a paradox. The less I felt for him, the more affectionate my behavior. A big hug first thing in the morning and last thing at night. Acting as his perennial sidekick at the synagogue, even though the mumbo-jumbo I kept hearing was an automatic turnoff. All the while yearning for Richard, my only father.

I'd pretty much forgotten about Weissensteiner by then. But

his face (Tommy Byrnes and the Joker) wasn't what floated back to me now. Instead, I kept seeing that scene in front of me, like a movie that keeps running with no ending in sight. The prisoner indistinct (it was only way afterwards that my mother doled out a few of my father's pictures to me), as he's being marched to the wall. The executioners' faces hidden by the turned-down brims of their Tyrolean hats. I kept seeing the guns raised, the body clenched and collapsing. Did I cry at the end of this nightly silent torment? I'm sure I did, when I thought of him lying on the ground in a red puddle. Followed by scenes where I broke into the jail at the very last minute. Then my one-man execution squad would put them up against the wall. Afterwards, the *coup de grâce* for each of them, with a bullet through the mouth. This magical wishlist of mine was as remote from fulfillment as having it in mind to fuck some movie star. You know there's not a chance in the world, but just the thought of it gives you a warm glow, deep in your gut.

One night, I dreamt that I was in St Marton to celebrate my Bar Mitzvah. In the next scene, my picture's in the paper, with a screaming headline (conveniently translated into English), "BAR MITZVAH BOY GOES BERSERK, MURDERS PATRIOT." There's an old picture of Weissensteiner, looking jaunty in his Nazi uniform. Another picture showing his coffin wrapped in a swastika flag, with people filing by. Cut to a jail cell. I'm being taken out to the wall – the same one – to be executed by firing squad. Because I'm a minor, they don't offer me a last cigarette. Instead, they let me keep my yarmulke and prayer shawl on until the very end. Ready, aim, fire. Like father, like son.

You must have heard about phantom pain. Your mind says your leg still burns or itches, but it's kidding you. The leg is gone, for good. Not that different from the way I felt. Richard was gone, but I kept feeling his presence. I never had much to go on, but I always imagined him smelling of apples, from walking through one orchard after another on the house calls he made on foot. And how he shaved with a straight razor, the only kind they used in those bygone days.

Now it's a different ballgame, and I'm about to face the real article. Meet and greet Herr W. and his henchboys, and make sure it is a brief – a very brief – acquaintance. Thanks to the ingenious instrument dozing in my carry-on luggage. Something to remember my father by.

In scientific research, you learn to be patient, let the facts come to you. This experiment is the exception. Bring on those results. I can't wait.

CHAPTER TWO
GRIEVING FOR EVA

February 1982

Nowadays I think about suicide much of the time. Not my own, God forbid! The idea of it. It's always gotten a bum rap, seems to me. Jumping off the sinking ship before the Captain gives the order is meant to be a sin. Look at it this way though: what's wrong with speeding up the process, DIY style? Think of what you save yourself. No walking the last mile with your ass hanging out of one of those hospital skivvies; doctors, about as much help as priests on Death Row, going through the motions with you. The dropping blood pressure rendezvousing with the soaring pulse; the 42nd Street and Broadway of leisurely dying. Fate? Destiny? Forget it. That's just the random dressed up as the predictable. But suicide is like making a reservation. No getting turned away at the door. Come right in, your end is waiting.

That's one way of looking at it. Still, it's not every day the brain gets to talk the body into killing itself. Depressives tend to do that. Psychiatrists lose sleep over it. Either because they're worried their patient is about to do it, or because she's done it already. Still, how about the ones who aren't depressed at all? Out of nowhere, they hang themselves, swallow gasoline and light a match, stick a plastic bag over their heads. Unpremeditated crimes against their nearest and dearest: themselves. But why?

My special interest in suicide goes back to the time when Eva, my old girlfriend from college, hung herself. On her fortieth birthday, no less. No warning signs, nothing to suggest she was about to do it. When we were twenty, we were about to get married, go away to graduate school together. Always a cheerful girl. Even after my mother broke up our romance by threatening me, a Jewish mamma's boy out of Central Casting, with "break that glass under the canopy, you're breaking my heart; besides, with all the excitement, I'm ready to drop dead anyway." Eva and I stayed close; but soon after, she married somebody else. An orphan, as it happened. The only time she ever got teary-eyed was when her favorite uncle, Alex was his name, came up in conversation. Always a happy go lucky guy; one night, while the rest of the family was at the movies, he slit his throat.

I spoke to her a week before she did it. She sounded the same as always. Her husband didn't notice anything either; at least that's what he told me afterwards. They were in the middle of getting dressed to go out, when she disappeared into the kitchen and strung herself up.

Friends and relatives of suicides are a guilty bunch. That's because they're always blaming themselves for not picking up the warning signals. Which was the way I felt too. But I also kept wondering, could she have had a backstairs romance with depression? Same as spending long afternoons fucking some secret guy. Wearing her despair out of sight, like naughty underwear. All the time calculating the height of the beam, the strength of the rope.

I was stuck. Even with a retrospectoscope – don't go running out looking to buy one; just a word doctors use for taking another, oftentimes guilty look at the past – I couldn't come up with any clues to her being a closet melancholic. So why did she do it? There had to be a reason.

For most of my life, my unconscious and I have just about been nodding acquaintances. Which is not to say we haven't enjoyed a collegial connection. If I send off a question last thing at night, the answer is there bright and early the next morning. Just another free of charge service from the city that never sleeps, aka my brain. One day, just as soon as I woke up, (the Eva quandary had kept me up most of the night), Harry Garner popped into my mind. Little Hitler moustache, magazines and papers sticking every which way out of suits that surrounded him like a poncho. He taught psychiatry to us first-year medical students, and one day we were interviewing a young girl who'd slit her wrists a couple of days before. Somebody pointed out she seemed pretty cheerful, considering. "Depression is not a requirement for doing away with yourself," Harry pointed out. I didn't know what he meant—then. A terrible dresser, but what an elegant talker, Harry.

After all those years, my unconscious led me right back to Harry. Who suggested I was missing the obvious. Eva hadn't left any clues, simply because there weren't any to leave. No depression; as far as I could tell, no motive either. And then there was her uncle, the one who slit his throat without warning. Close relatives like that, killing themselves. Did they share some wild gene that pushed them into it? But how does a gene like that work? It doesn't just go around whispering suggestions in your ear to kill yourself. There's got to be a middleman somewhere, I kept thinking. Some tie-in that forces the hand to turn on the gas, makes the legs climb up onto the windowsill.

Random thoughts in between grieving for Eva. Ours was a 19th century kind of affair; all talk, very little action. Mostly sitting around, holding hands in candlelit cafés on MacDougal Street. Lingually deprived, dry-as-blotter-paper kisses, the length of the elevator trip (too short, why didn't she live in the Empire State Building?) to her family's apartment on the third floor. No consummation, not even memories of some passionate, fumbling *touche-pipi*. My twenty-year-old self's feelings arrested in time, like a dried-out flower in a glass case.

CHAPTER THREE
MY CBD

1948

My apartment looks like the Junior Assistant storeroom at Barnes & Noble. Dark even on bright days. The only touch of color: at night you can just about see the red Pepsi-Cola sign flashing from across the river. Lots of industrial shelving loaded with books, the rest piled up on the floor and even in the kitchen cabinets. (I've never counted how many there are; must be at least two thousand.) It's gotten so bad, my landlord is trying to evict me. Somebody told him I was a bookworm, so he thought he'd put two and two together. There are some insect problems in the apartment beneath mine, so (if you ever met him, you'd agree he doesn't look like much of a reader) he's convinced my books are spawning the worms which then work their way downstairs. We have a date in Housing Court in a couple of months.

For a long time now, I've suffered from a sickness having to do with books. My parents were the rare Austrian Jews who were allowed to take their entire library with them when the Nazis forced them out of the country. Three cookbooks (one of them devoted entirely to 19th century logistics in the production of *Apfelstrudel*) and a volume of the collected *Max und Moritz* stories (sort of *The Katzenjammer Kids*, but in German.) Even those small pickings were kept on a shelf I couldn't reach. The phonebook was handier – they kept it with the galoshes in the hall closet.

This need to read led to unexpected consequences when I was around seven or eight. I found myself going over the weekly limit at the lending library. Also filching magazines from Ye Tobacconist around the corner from our house. Meanwhile ordering free come-on copies of the Book of the Month Club under an assumed name. Hoodwinking my parents by going under covers with my flashlight, reading into the early mornings.

Pretty soon, my mother noticed I was getting thinner, and began to pay what I thought was extraordinary attention to the sheets on my bed. When people are desperate, they turn – a lot of the time misguidedly – to their doctors. A quick fix is what they hope for. What to eat, what not to eat; not enough vitamins, too many; is the tap water filled with toxins? My mother presented me to Dr Gardner, our family doctor. Talking as if I wasn't there, she kept coming back to this one word. To me, it sounded like "anonymous." (I realized only afterwards, it was onanism they were talking about.) Holy shit, I thought, the Book of the Month Club finally got wise to me; maybe I wasn't so anonymous after all.

When the kindly old doc took me into his examining room and asked me to drop my pants, that really scared me. I was convinced the Club was about to take revenge for the way I tricked it for freebies. Just as I was ready to confess and offer a deal – I'd give back all their books, plus a few of my own to sweeten the pot – the doctor checked what I had down there. That took all of thirty seconds. "The ground is pretty bare. Just a little maple sapling, but right now it's too fragile to reach to the sky. Don't expect any syrup to come out of there for quite a while," he told my mother. All the magazines in his waiting room had something to do with the preservation of our precious forests.

You'd think my mother would give up after the reassuring visit with Dr Gardner. But she wouldn't, so we ended up seeing Dr Kleban, a child psychiatrist. When I first saw him, I thought there must be some mistake. Pediatricians oftentimes look like kids. Short, with that about-to-be-spanked-any-minute look. So, it was just one step further for my child psychiatrist to remind me of a disturbed kid. Couldn't sit still, his oversized tortoise-shell glasses bobbing up and down from his blinking eyes to his flaring nostrils. Still, he was good at getting me to *kvetch* about what was bothering me. So I let my pants down (figuratively this time around) and explained about this need of mine to beg, borrow or steal books.

It turned out my sickness has a name. "Compulsive Bibliophilia Disorder" (CBD for short) is what he called it. In my experience, patients don't give a shit about diagnosis. It's the prognosis they're after: is the boo-boo about to go away, are they going to live to tell the tale? In my case, there was (and still is) no treatment. You don't die from it, but it doesn't go away either. And it's not just about reading. That's a big part of it for sure. But just holding and sniffing the book before I buy it (sometimes I have to pinch one if there's no other way to make it mine) and then carrying it home like some precious conquest, is as much of a kick as setting my eyes on what's inside. Besides, there's the flavor of the books themselves. I like to roll my tongue over the bindings, and taste what they have to offer. Something like running wine over your palate. The combo of glue and stiff paper unique for each one. Not exactly the "taste in books" the literati get off on; just my way of snuggling up even closer to what I can't resist in the first place.

CHAPTER FOUR
ARLENE I

August 1981

Not that I turned into a wallflower after I broke up with Eva.
Jewish boys who are about to become doctors are objects of
intense interest to both mothers and daughters. A kind of jungle
tom-tom announced my arrival on this particular scene. Distant
relatives who had not been heard from for practically forever, and
fellow parishioners of my parents at Temple Israel in Fort Lee,
all clamored to fix me up with their particular recommendation.
Who, according to them, was invariably "beautiful," "a wonderful
human being," and whose parents "aren't exactly poor, you catch
my drift?" It wasn't for lack of trying. I followed up on every lead,
but over the years the experience was like picking my way through
a buffet. A taste here, a taste there. Nobody pretending it's a
real meal, but it does fill you up; for the time being at least. All I
ended up with were souvenir cocktail napkins and multicolored
toothpicks. A waste of time all around. No wonder the amateur
marriage brokers gave up on me.

By then, I was like the guy who's always the last to leave the
party. Hoping to snare the girl who'd had no takers all evening.
This freelance mooning around was no more successful than my
dealings with the candidates from the Temple Israel connection.

I was at a dead end. If life wasn't totally passing me by, it wasn't giving me a promising pat on the back either.

New York streets in August give you that special feeling, like it's carnival time in Rio. The smell, to start out with. Dog shit, gas fumes, hot rubber on about-to-melt asphalt, reheated uncollected garbage, and the vapor (what's it made of anyway?) that's belched up by the storm drains. Also the sweat, the wet stickiness of your pants reminding you of the good old days when it was OK to piss in them. Walk around like that long enough, and a primitive part of your brain gets called front and center. The one that doesn't turn up its nose at putrid smells or slippery-slidey skin. Watch it skillfully shake all the ingredients I just mentioned into an erotic cocktail. Just before serving, add anybody, anybody at all (a complete stranger usually works best), and you have the perfect concoction for one hot night.

Which is exactly what happened to me. It came out of nowhere, but turned out to make a big difference in my life. Late one evening, I was walking back to my house from the County Hospital. We'd spent a few hours removing blood clots and pieces of bone from the brains of three ex-friends. They'd been aiming a baseball bat at each other's heads, in a struggle over a bottle of rum. I was tired, but there was no way I could miss a group of about ten or fifteen girls standing around in front of the building across from where I live. There was a hum coming from their general direction, the kind of background choral music made by women in groups. "Hey guys, we're having a fine time without you, thankyouverymuch. But if you can't stand to stay away, just follow your ears."

Once in a while, looking out of my window, I'd seen one or two going in and out of what looked like a dormitory. But this was the first time I saw them in a bunch. They turned out to be student social workers from a college in upstate New York. They were here, learning how to find a place to live for ninety-year-olds dumped by their families, or who to contact about getting work for amputees with five kids to feed. That's the kind of practice they get in their three months at the County, before going back to their college for more coursework. One man chatting up fifteen women has it made. Fifteen men chatting up one woman – watch out, I don't have to tell you. Still, a lone male is automatically a mascot, he's not considered dangerous. At least while he's taking his time figuring out which of the ladies he's about to rip away from the pack. As far as I was concerned, there were four or five standing there who made my shortlist right away. Trouble was, I couldn't tell them apart. Denim shorts, halter tops. Very sexy in my opinion, because since they're evidently not wearing anything underneath those, could that be true for the shorts also? The latter possibility being even more outstandingly sexy in my opinion. Besides, they all had kinky, curly hair.

It was like trying to choose a pup at a kennel. What I really wanted was to take them all home with me. Just a passing thought, as gymnastic and mathematical possibilities rose up before my eyes. I had to choose – but quick – before they all scurried away thinking collectively I'd rejected each of them individually. A last-resort look gave me my out. Kinky-haired they all were, but one of them was special in that department. Her shiny, wet ringlets reminded me of a sketch I once saw of Louis XIV's wig after a thorough rinsing. Complimented her on the coiffure, using the Sun King as a personal reference. That did the trick. In time, the others went on their way like chorus girls after a nothing-doing tryout. Somebody with my history can't afford to burn bridges. Before they took off, I came up with an emergency party favor.

A blanket invitation to watch a real live brain operation – as my special guests – someday very soon.

That's how I first met Arlene I. Unforgettable, that's what she was. Starting with that night, I never stopped discovering novel things about her. For instance, how she managed to keep her palms dry, though her fingers felt like they had just been lightly dipped in something creamy. Also, there were the ringlets pouring down her neck, which somehow stayed at a respectful distance from her forehead. In other words, none of that annoying, don't see how she can see straight, all the time pursing her lips to blow her hair upward, sheepdog look. Also, contact lenses in place. So, no embarrassing optometric faux pas – my frames or yours? Things got even better when she helped me unravel something that was always a puzzle for me: the inner workings of a halter top.

But these were only preliminaries to the main event. That's when I first smelled that scent. A bouquet rather; equal parts lilac and tie dye, rising up from a triangular area – roughly halfway between the knees and the belly button – covered by her slightly moist denim shorts. Move over Marcel, this wasn't just a question of nostalgia for long-ago madeleines. Also, no connection whatsoever with the shellfish, kelp, and wet rocks pussyfooting around engaged in by authorities on female smells. No, what made it so alluring was the outcome of the chemical reaction between the denim and the dampness. For all I know, old Levi Strauss packed some aphrodisiac or other into his pants which requires the addition of a special fluid (provided by the consumer) to come up to speed.

It was like experimenting with airplane glue or cocaine. Never tried the stuff myself. But "Where has this been all my life," and "When and where can I get more of it," that's what I kept thinking after my very first exposure to Arlene I's fumes. I wasn't experimenting. I was already hooked.

In science, you learn to check and recheck, make sure you got it right the first time. That's why I put the bulletin from my nose to the test with the other four senses. No need to go into detail about touching and looking and tasting. But hearing? Every time I rubbed the denim, degree of sprinkle already discussed, gently over her pubic bone – that's the one belly dancers throw out at you like a satellite launch at Cape Canaveral – there was kind of a ripply sound. Like when you're smoothing out a velvet curtain after it's been caught in the rain. Anyway, all my five senses agreed. This was something special. After a few nightly shuttles over to my place, Arlene I and I ended up with an *amitié amoureuse*. The ties of a loving friendship without the noose of an affair.

By the time September came around, Arlene I invited the other ones, the chorus line rejects, up to my apartment. They still looked a lot alike to me. Maybe not their faces, but their frizzy hair and those denims they wore like a uniform. By that time of year, it was either long skirts – the nostalgic, peasant look – or jeans.

Why the frizzy hair? Early on, I did what's called a controlled study. Frizzy hair, no denim – none of the usual effect. The other way around, same thing. No question the two went together. But how? Could frizzy-haired social workers have a specific chemical circulating in their blood that works as a catalyst – a fixer – which puts the denim-moistness connection over the top?

As I was sitting there looking around at Arlene I and the others, I saw the future, bright and clear. After the girls left, I had a talk with Arlene I. Her tour of duty at the County was almost over, and she was due to go back upstate in a few days. Neither of us had brought up the subject of if – or when – we were going to see each other again. Going cold turkey, so early in my addiction, would have been bad news. That's why I felt it was OK to pop the question about transition arrangements for Max.

I never expected her to be anything other than a sexual democrat. I'm not talking politics, just equal opportunity for all. Think of it: she agreed to pick out her successor for the shuttle! A candidate from the chorus line, Arlene II. Same basic equipment in the curls and denim department. Also, her exhalations turned out to be identical to Arlene I's. But in other ways the two girls were a lot different. Arlene I would slink across the street late at night with a *babushka* hiding her face. Very secretive. Didn't want the doormen and security guards on either end to do a positive ID on her. Arlene II liked the daytime. She'd come over first thing in the morning, naked under a trench coat made of –you guessed it–denim. Every once in a while, she'd even come to the lab in the same getup. I know some women like to walk around without panties in place. But nothing on at all? What if there was a sudden windstorm, or she was hit by a car? Arlene II used to tell me that walking around naked, being the only one to know, with the chance of exposure at any minute, that's what turned her on.

When Arlene II left, she appointed her successor. And that's how it went on. More Arlenes, not to speak of Eileens, Ilenes, Ellens, Elenas. The whole scheme worked out just fine.

I look at myself as a faithful guy. Maybe not in the same way as men who spend all their life with just one woman. They're more in the category of marathon runners, with that spent, pained, exhausted look as they come up to the finish line. I'm more of a sprinter. Giving it everything I've got over short distances, one race at a time.

CHAPTER FIVE

HOW FIDO TEITELBAUM CHANGED MY LIFE

February 1984

I'm walking on the way from my lab at the County to the weekly meeting of the Department at the Schultz. It used to be called University Hospital, but in the Seventies a mogul called Schultz offered three million bucks to plaster his name all over the pile of grayish brick. Cheaper than buying a basketball team, he must have thought. Wrong! With a team—even if it's a loser—there's a win once in a while. But hospitals? War zones all of them, nonstop. No peace, no victory, not even a truce—ever. The combatants lying there, slowly decomposing in the heat exhaled by those whirring, beeping, scintillating robots keeping tabs on when—they couldn't care less why, or where it is we all end up—everybody's going to die. Also, a pipeline runs through every one of them, pushing along a dark, smelly liquid. It's shit, the universal lubricant, collected and delivered from top to bottom and from side to side. All the time, no let-up. Too bad you can't run cars on it. Otherwise we'd have the energy crisis fixed in a jiffy. So, was this a fitting memorial for Schultz?

It was a heist. Schultz never paid a dime. Something about unexpected losses at his boutique junkyards. What could they do about it, the too trusting Trustees? Not much. Schultz (University)

Hospital it was going to stay. Except there's no way you can hear a parenthesis. So now it's going to sound forever like Schultz has a university too, not just a hospital.

As I walk, the East River is rushing by on my right. On some days, when it's misty enough, the tugboats turn into war canoes defending the coast of Long Island City, across the way. An Optical Joke. To my left, a fenced-in playing field with a dust storm for a floor. Inside, the little inmates from the County Psycho getting their daily airing, the pills they're fed like mother's milk making their movements herky-jerky, like puppets.

Three years before – on the 4th of July – I was making my way in the opposite direction, from the Schultz to the County. All the other adults had gone off to their weekend houses in St Bart's, or even on a quick visit to a fancy resort in the Indian Ocean. I was on call for the entire neurosurgery service, which meant I was the one available in case one of our patients ran into trouble. I was about to cross through the Schultz Emergency Room to get to the back door, which leads to a shortcut to the County, down the road. As I walked into the ER, I heard yelling and screaming coming from one of the cubicles. So far, nothing unusual. Patients and/or relatives, refusing to believe you can be fine one minute and down the drain the next. Which is like arguing with a cop over a ticket.

I took a look behind the curtain, and came upon a man and a woman desperately pulling a large brown dog onto the examining table. At the same time, a couple of determined-looking nurses were doing their best to push him off. The dog was not making a sound, his four legs sticking straight up in the air, only taking an occasional shallow breath. No question he was in a coma. I took a quick history, and found out that Fido, a three-year-old chocolate Labrador, had fallen down a whole flight of stairs an hour before, and landed on his head. A few minutes later, he became unresponsive. In a panic, his owners, carrying the dog between them, flagged down a cab and asked the driver to take them to the Animal Medical Center. The driver must not have heard the first part. He took them to the Schultz ER instead. I talked the nurses into leaving the dog on the table, so I could examine him. One of his pupils was much larger than the other. That, together with the coma, meant he had a fast-growing blood clot pressing on his brain. It was too late to do a CT scan to confirm what I was thinking. In the time it would take to schedule and perform, he was sure to be dead. I quickly sent to the OR for the instrument pack used for neurosurgical emergencies. A few minutes later, I was drilling a hole on the side of the head where the clot was likely to be. A spray of blood came pouring out, and the dog's breathing improved almost at once. A half hour later, he opened his eyes. He was coming out of the coma.

I've seen some grateful patients' relatives in my time, when things turned out the way everybody hoped. The patient better, smiles all around. The family throwing their arms around you, kissing your hands. On the other hand, if the results are bad, you don't know what to do first. Run to the bathroom, or make sure your malpractice insurance is up to date. The owners of this dog were different. As soon as he began to wake up, they both began to sob. Fido was licking everybody he could get his paws on, and his owners couldn't stop hugging and kissing him. It was obvious we had to get the dog out of the ER ASAP. The shit was sure to hit the fan, sooner rather than later. Lucky it was a holiday weekend. If not, one of those chickenshit hospital administrators – they don't know from beans what makes medicine tick – would already have been nosing around, having conniptions about how you can't take care of dogs in a people Emergency Room, etc., etc. It ended up with the owners, Teitelbaum is their name, taking my patient home after I'd arranged for a couple of off-duty neurosurgical ICU nurses to keep an eye on him. An oxygen tank and a heart monitor were delivered within the hour to one of the old Georgian mansions up on Murray Hill where Fido and his folks lived. In the end, the dog got the best postop care – animal or human – of anybody in the metropolitan area that holiday weekend. Which, as everybody knows, is the worst time to get sick, since the fledglings are just out of medical school and are – without exception – wet behind the ears.

Within a day, Fido was back to normal. Jumping up and down, pissing all over the oxygen tank. He must have thought it was that rarest of objects, an indoor fire hydrant. By the time I took out his stitches a few days later, it was time to say goodbye. That's when Arnold and Marie – which by this time they insisted I call them – invited me for a farewell drink. They'd done their homework. They'd already looked into the best way they could show their appreciation "for bringing our Fido back to us." With that in mind, they'd had a talk about me with The Chief. They'd found him "charming." Which suggested to me he smelled their hundred million bucks – the amount Arnold had gotten from the sale of his electronics business – as soon as they came in the door. The upshot? They were endowing the Fido Teitelbaum Professorship of Neurosurgery. Meaning they were going to donate a few million, which would be invested, so the income could pay the salary of a professor and the cost of his research. Plus a nice chunk for the Department. And the first Fido Teitelbaum Professor? Who else but me? The only catch being I had to turn forty-five before it was official. That's what The Chief told them were the rules of the Department. News to me. He then suggested himself for the job (though he already held two other endowed professorships) if they were in a hurry, since he already fit the age requirements. They wouldn't hear of it, since it was me, and no one else, who'd saved the life of their Fido. They were putting up the money now, but it was to be held in escrow, with the interest going to the Department until I came of age.

CHAPTER SIX
THE CHIEF

February 1984

The conference rooms at the Schultz are all inside, like the cheaper staterooms on a cruise ship. No windows, no sunlight. Like in Las Vegas, where it's always a guess if it's day or night. Besides, in these closed spaces, there's no fresh air, winter or summer. What you get instead is cold, recycled wind. Pollution, hospital style. Your lungs getting a whiff of what everybody else just coughed up or belched out.

There are little pockets the wind never gets to. My first impression as I walk into the weekly neurosurgical conference: a familiar aroma that hits you in waves. The first one seeming to vaporize out of the walls. That's what a long-sealed burial chamber must smell like; insistent but not overpowering, the sharpness gone out of it. Generations of trainees leaving us a sepulchral hello.

Where the second wave comes from – it reminds you of onion soup, but hits the nose like a punch – is obvious. The gamy odor of slept-in scrub suits released by last night's on-call group. Clipboards held to their defenseless chests like shields; heads lolling like some *Lubyanka* guest after an all-nighter. Sitting close by, but worlds apart: the Chief Resident, magnificent in his spotless white coat set off by the blue and gold Princeton tie. The *Judenrat* appointed to keep the perspiring aspirants running and panting after the mechanical rabbit.

Da Nang Bill O'Foaleolain, The Chief, is presiding. Lab coat over scrubs; dog tags gilded like a baby's first shoes, glinting in the yellowish light coming out of the fluorescents overhead. OR cap worn at a rakish angle. No Major's oak leaves pinned to it? Must have left the insignia at home by mistake. Shiny combat boots complete the ensemble. Two years in the Army, three months in Vietnam. Ten years out, he's still playing soldier. And it's not just the getup he wears. How about some of the stuff he writes? "Neurosurgery: A Military Metaphor," for starters. Published in that right-wing rag, *Annals of Patriotic Medicine*, a few years ago. After that, it only gets worse.

He's a classic case of cardio-cerebral disjunction. A fancy way of saying his heart's still out there in the glory days of Da Nang, but the rest of him stays planted in his duplex penthouse on Sutton Place. His reentry into civilian life smooth; no crash landing for this Vietnam vet.

Good to know he's not perfect. Of all things, it's his name that's a problem. Wouldn't be in Ireland, where having lots of vowels is nothing special. Even here it's not a big deal, considering almost everybody goes by the unisex pseudonym of "Hi" or "Hey" anyway. But on early morning neurosurgical rounds, you can't blame a patient for wanting to address his doctor by his real name, not that moronic diminutive "Doc." That's where O'Foaleolain can be a real handicap. A lot of patients needed emergency testing right after rounds – slurring of speech, involuntary movements of the muscles of the face. A stroke overnight? A worsening of the tumor? You'd think The Chief would have changed his name, made things easier for everybody. But no, only Jews and transsexuals do that. You leave for vacation as Marvin, come back as Mary-Ellen. Or, everybody knows you as Yossi Farfelmacher, all of a sudden you're James Fenton.

I'm in charge of neurosurgical training at the County. That's like being a lifeguard. Just another pretty face when nobody is drowning, but if one of our fledglings is about to knock a patient off by doing too much or too little, I'm your man. Most of the time, I get them out of trouble. But if I can't, it's our collective ass; the fledglings' and mine. Coliseum time at the weekly conference. Chief snarling. The smell of blood in the air.

Not that I operate much anymore. I lost my taste for it a while ago. Finding out what the brain has on its mind was beginning to make more sense to me than cutting heads open for a living. A short time before Eva's death, I'd put the final touches on my research project. I was about to do a house-to-house census of the brain, searching for spaces reserved for genius. Beethoven, Babe Ruth, Duke Ellington: did they get to skip the preliminaries because they were born with the right wiring for the limelight? The spaces I was about to explore are called "special centers." They're the UFOs of brain research. Meaning they may not even exist. And even if they do, talking the brain into unlocking its own secrets is about as easy as getting to interview the little guy with the antenna growing out of the top of his head.

I waited all morning for the routine stuff to end. The morbidity and mortality report, meaning who we made worse and who died on our watch. Statistics. You read them like a batting average, except the lower the percentage, the better you're doing. Also, funding issues and complimentary letters about what a wonderful department we are. What came next were the updates on research done by the faculty. These usually gave me the willies. Reminded me of my abortive hitch in the Boy Scouts. Troop 166 used to meet every week in a temple in Fort Lee. At least once every session, we were supposed to jump up on a rope and climb it all the way to the ceiling. The first time, my palms were already sweaty. For good reason; I'm a terrible klutz. As expected, my hands promptly slid off the rope. I fell on my ass. Not only once, but three times in a row. After that, I stayed on the ground, my face as red as my palms, while the rest of the troop scampered up there in their brown uniforms. To me they looked more like Hitler Youth, the higher they climbed. After that, I hid out in one of the stalls in the men's room, as soon as my early warning system–a big-time cramp in the stomach–notified me that jungle gym was ready to start. Thirty years on, I was still getting ready to hide out in the toilet whenever it came time to report on my suicide project.

By this time, I'd long ago put Beethoven and the Bambino on the back burner. Ever since I understood that Eva might not have planned to kill herself, I'd started hunting for some special area that can trigger suicide on its own. Located in some dull suburb of the brain, one of those nondescript places you realize was a bomb factory only after the neighborhood blows up. I had no proof; it was just a remote hunch. But how often can you tell the same story without proof? Time after time, I sat there in my own logorrhea; the smell of defeat keeping everybody far away from me. But that day, I couldn't wait to spill the beans. Not all the beans–just enough to make people sit up and listen.

Akbar Kurastami, known to all as Persian Pete, had the floor. Black hair slicked back, merging at the neck with grey curls rising like seaweed from the back of his collar. Tight-fitting, double-breasted pinstripe suit, dark grey silk shirt and a tie with lots of pink in it. With that outfit, he could have done it all. Sell anything from underage girls to over-the-hill washing machines. As usual, he was going on and on about his pet subject, the post cingulate cortex. A part of the brain that's a lunar landscape, off the tourist route of even such adventurous travelers as cancers and ready-to-pop blood vessels. Persian Pete is the world expert on this area, and he's convinced there is oil under that particular desert. Male mice have a penis which is half as long as their entire bodies. So he removed the post cingulate cortex from a bunch of mice – post mortem – and mashed up what he got out. When you're doing experiments with mice, to get an erection going, you have to use an electrical probe. For them to get a spontaneous hard-on, they need to be in the company of their female counterparts, back in the communal cage. So he injected the solution he'd made from the post cingulate cortexes, hoping to make the live mice rise and shine. Nothing doing. He then tried different dosages, also different liquids for the solutions. Still, nothing doing.

You'd think that would put an end to the project. Wrong! In research, not knowing is as good as knowing, maybe even better. You can make a whole career out of coming up with progress reports about your lack of progress. He kept beating the subject to death in that crooning voice. The accent a cocktail of French, plus a light hint of American, with occasional weekends in Cairo thrown in. I just wished he'd shut up.

Besides, I had some scores to settle with him. Whenever he could, he tried to make mincemeat of my project. "Max, this just doesn't make sense," "Max, you can't be serious." That's what I really needed, to be made a laughing stock in front of the Department. While his research was more "serious"… trying to give mice a hard on?

And then there was the matter of Rosie, The Chief's red-headed secretary. She was one of those women who send out a prologue before they walk into a room, and an epilogue as they're leaving. One long-ago Christmas, I asked her to be my date at the party the Department throws every year. As soon as I mentioned it, she put on this wistful puss. Eyes a little moist, her face getting pink. No "sorry," no thanks for the invitation. Came right out with it. "Akbar (what's this with calling a senior surgeon by his first name?) and I have plans for the evening." I could right away see that kissing under the mistletoe was not going to be at the very top of their agenda. I was plenty pissed off at Pete after that turndown. You're entitled to ask why, but I don't have a good answer for that. The truth is, there was no reason for him to know about my invitation to Rosie. But it was still his fault because he was always standing in my way. Women after him, never after me. The OR nurses falling over each other to scrub with him, long discussions with the prettiest of our girl students in his office, door closed. I was on real short rations then—I hadn't met my student social workers yet, who promptly pulled me out of these particular doldrums—while he had a glut on his hands. It wouldn't have killed him to be more generous, share the wealth. Instead, he kept all the goodies to himself.

No way I was ever going to forget what he did to me.

When my turn came, The Chief didn't even bother to call me up to the lectern. He just looked in my direction, and, using that special tone he could pull out in an instant for giving patients bad news (feeling your pain but oh, ever so glad I'm not you), asked: "You got anything new, Max?"

I didn't answer right away. He was just going to go on to the next speaker when I got up and walked to the front of the room, dropping my slides off with the projectionist along the way.

CHAPTER SEVEN
THE ME

May 1983

The New York City Medical Examiner's Office, the ME, has its own blue brick building in the no-man's land between the County and the Schultz. That's where the business of death is transacted – the lobby filled with funeral directors milling around the secretary in charge of dispensing death certificates, waiting to get their particular show on the road ASAP. A couple of years ago, I started going up to the autopsy rooms to schmooze about suicides with the staff. I told them what I was looking for; an abnormal spot in the brain that in some way made people knock themselves off. They were polite, but I could tell they were pretty dubious about what I was getting at. Still, they began calling me whenever a suicide was brought in for autopsy. I'd look at the brain with the pathologist while he was dissecting it. We never found anything out of the way. Ditto with looking under the microscope, even with special stains to check for abnormal cells or blood vessels. Some of the brains we examined belonged to people whose stories were similar to Eva's. No depression, fine until the last moment, but they still ended up hanging themselves or slitting their throats. Over time, I began thinking of them as the "amateurs." Nothing like those regular customers of psychiatric clinics, "suicide risks" they're called, the long-time depressives and schizophrenics. Those are the "professionals." They know what they're doing. So far, no way of telling one group from another. I'd have to dig deeper.

Around that time, one of the first MRI's in the city was installed at the Schultz. For me it was a godsend. I found out pretty quick how good the technology is at finding tiny tumors or weak blood vessels in remote parts of the brain, the kind of out-of-the-way conditions a C-T scan – or even the microscope – misses sometimes. Much in demand, the MRI was in use from early morning until late at night. But I had a Trojan horse on the MRI service: Murray, one of our old trainees, who'd washed out of the program because his hands kept shaking whenever he scrubbed with The Chief. Pissed Da Nang Bill off. According to him, when you're working on the brain, there's no room for distraction. You're feeling anxious, your bladder's about to bust, an itch in your balls – forget about it. So now, Murray was a happy voyeur, a radiologist, looking instead of doing. Hands so steady I'd let him carry a bucket of nitroglycerine for me anytime. When I explained to him what I was looking for, he offered to keep the MRI lit for me after hours. That's how I found myself walking into the sub-basement of the Schultz some evenings, carrying a canvas bag with Domino's Pizza plastered all over it. What it actually contained was the newly removed brain of a suicide, which I'd borrowed from the Assistant Medical Examiner who had just done the autopsy. It would have been everybody's ass if what we were doing had leaked out. But who's going to be suspicious of a guy who's innocently bringing over a pizza to share with his old friend Murray at the end of a long day?

It's a lot easier to do an MRI on a brain that's separated from its owner. Pacemakers, credit cards, watches, the stuff that makes the magnet go haywire–no problem. Same goes for the panic some patients get into when they find themselves locked into that tight metal cylinder. First they fidget; then they start yelling, begging to be let out. It takes a lot longer to do the job that way. But with the brain on its own; out of the pizza bag in a jiffy, onto the spot where the head usually rests. Then the twenty-minute bombardment (no kidding, it sounds like a war in there) by the magnetic waves. At the end, you have the most intimate snapshots of the brain you could hope for.

The first two brains I brought over showed nothing special on the MRI. Afterwards, I checked the histories of their late owners. Ten attempted suicides between them, plus volumes of notes to show for their many visits to mental hygiene clinics. People get to put their heads inside one of these psychiatric laundromats for fifteen minutes every couple of weeks, courtesy of New York City. They're supposed to do a wash and dry of your brain. Clean out whatever is bothering you. Psychoanalysis? The exact opposite. Look for help in that direction, you get to splash around in your own dirt. As long and as often as the insurance company or your father can afford it.

A couple of days later, I brought a brain from a new suicide over to Murray. As I was hurrying my pizza bag and its contents back to the ME, I got an urgent message from him. He'd found something.

CHAPTER EIGHT
THE SUICIDE CENTER

July 1983

The locus ceruleus is a pile of nerve cells that looks like a blue birthmark. There's one on each side of the pons, the bridge which connects the brain to the spinal cord.

"That's the left locus ceruleus," Murray said, his hand shaking a little. What he was pointing to was a dime-sized spot, kind of transparent looking, on the MRI slices coming down from the brain and working their way to the spinal cord. "Nothing wrong with this one. Now I'm going to scroll over to the other side."

Pretty soon the right locus ceruleus drifted into view and Murray magnified it, like in the movies when a train or a plane starts out as a speck and comes toward you, getting bigger and bigger all the time. Murray didn't have to explain. Same outline as the one on the left, but there was something different about it. It looked like a tarnished dime, mottled and gray. Not blue.

"Never seen anything like it," he said. Now I knew why his hand was shaking. "See how it stays the same, the deeper I scroll into the pons?" Boy, did I want to believe him. But until we checked with the microscope, the strange right locus might have nothing to do with a suicide center at all.

A few minutes later, Murray and I were standing in one of the smaller autopsy rooms of the ME. The brain I'd just brought back was sitting on a dissection table, looking like a plump white cat, head burrowed under its paws. On the walk over there together, I began to feel more upbeat. Hadn't I figured my center might be hiding out in a dull suburb like the pons? Besides, it's common knowledge that there's a private detective in the brain, specializing in confidential matters like anxiety and fear. And who's that? The locus ceruleus, as it happens. All in all, I couldn't think of a better place for a mysterious outfit like a suicide center to sublet a quiet little apartment.

The pathologist on duty was Peter Bishop. Born in England, trained at Hopkins. Young-looking, with a red face and prematurely white hair. One of those forever boyish Brits. In my mind they're always in shorts and rugby shirts. Lucky he was around that night. The sharpest of them all, but an expert at taking the piss. One of the blood sports of his native country; not only putting the victim down, but focusing on the part of him that can least afford it. As Murray was putting the MRI images on the viewbox, "please don't let him shake," I thought. When we started looking at the pictures, Peter began to address him in measured tones and perfect pitch. As if he was reading the Magna Carta to an English-as-a-third-language immigrant. "And what have we here…" he asked, pointing first to the viewbox, then to the brain glistening under the surgical overhead light, "…art imitating death?"

Never was so little said in so many words. (Unconfirmed attribution: Churchill, Winston. 1941.) Before he could go into one of those endless riffs of his, I jumped in. "Cut the shit, Peter. Just look at what Murray has to show you."

Peter was a quick study. I don't think he'd ever seen an MRI before, but he understood right away what we were trying to get at. All business now, he began his dissection. A few minutes later, he showed us what we'd come to see. The locus ceruleus, the blue spot; first the right one, and then its twin on the left. Both looked normal. They never do microscopics of the locus at the ME; no call for it. But this was a different story. Either the microscopics were going to tie up with what was on the MRI, or Murray and I had a lot of explaining to do.

The next morning I got up even earlier than usual. Didn't sleep well anyway; too much handicapping what the microscopics were going to show. When I got to the ME around seven, Peter was already there. With his arms hugging the microscope, he looked like one of those morons who keep a stranglehold on their girls as they walk them down the street. As soon as he saw me, he put on the teaching head so we could look at the slides together. First he showed me cuts of the left locus, then the right.

"No question about it," he said, sounding less Old Britannia for a change, and more Newyorknewyork urgent.

"The left one looks completely normal. But can you see the difference? The right is darker, and its nerve cells are dissolved, with their walls all broken up." He was right. You didn't have to be a pathologist to understand what he was talking about. "What do you make of it?" I asked.

"These changes are quite specific. I've seen them elsewhere in the brain in just two situations."

"And they are…?"

Peter got up and began to rummage through his bookcase. After a while, he pulled a reprint of an article out of a manila envelope.

"A few years ago, I got to study the brains of people executed in the electric chair at Sing Sing. Look at the pictures of the slides. And here are some I took from the microscopics of people who

51

were killed by lightning. Now give our locus ceruleus another look. Can't tell them apart, can you, except that they're in a different part of the brain? What this all means," Peter continued, "is that the severe damage to the nerve cells all comes from the same source. An electrical burn."

"How do you know that for sure?"

"Because part of the brain fries after it's struck by lightning."

"Yes, so?"

"Well then if the brains of the ones who died in the electric chair, and of people who were struck by lightning, and now the locus ceruleus of our case," he waved in the general direction of the microscope, "all show the same changes, it stands to reason that…"

"They all come from electrical burns."

"Very good," he said, as if talking to an idiot child.

Maybe what Murray had was catching. My own hands shook a bit too as I was thumbing through the chart, looking for the sheet that gave some information about this suicide's past. Sometimes you draw a blank. No relatives or friends, no clinic notes, found floating in the river without ID. But I was in luck. Forty-year-old Caucasian housewife with two teenage children. Husband a technical writer working at home. No previous attempts, no history of depression. Found dead in her bathtub, early the morning before. Slit her wrists during the night, hour undetermined.

The story put her in with the amateurs, and her right locus ceruleus was somehow involved in an electrical fire. I'd have to come up with a solid explanation for the fire. Was it an overloaded circuit, or a spark at the wrong time, that started things off?

CHAPTER NINE
I SPILL THE BEANS

February 1984

The Chief's earlobes were getting redder by the second. To anybody who's ever been around him, that means the early stages of pissed off. Doesn't appreciate surprises at his conferences. Makes it look like he doesn't have 100% of everything under his control, 100% of the time. I soon realized I'd have to make my pitch very convincing, to avoid a five or six on the Richter scale from him. Persian Pete looking at me sideways. Bryce Gillespie, the Chief Resident—the way WASPs name their kids, could just as well be Gillespie Bryce—looking thoughtful. In a holding pattern until he can figure out what facial expression works best for his plot to become The Chief's associate.

But the first case was no fluke. After that one, we'd gotten three more. Same deformed right locus on MRI and microscopic, amateurs from the looks of their history sheets.

This time around, nobody could accuse me of only talking a good game. I showed the slides and MRIs of all four. Four sudden suicides, four abnormal MRIs and microscopics of not just any locus, just the right one. I was onto something the brain was planning to keep to itself forever. They knew it, I knew it.

A few lousy slides and I was rehabilitated. Richter scale aborted.

Chief calm; Chief Resident outright grinning, nudging his sleepy charges to "show some interest, for crissake." Pete's right thumb bobbing up and down like in a vigorous session of you know what. Happy for me? No way. At that moment everybody there was calculating how to hitch a ride with me. And even how to make off with the car, while I was busy taking a leak by the side of the road.

It's always good to hold something back. Women know that. Give it all up at the beginning? A sure way to get treated like shit. That's why I didn't spill all the beans at once. Makes everybody wait for the other shoe to drop. Drives them nuts.

CHAPTER TEN

THE PARTHENON

February 1984

After the weekly conference, on the way to my office at the County, I make my first visit of the day to the Parthenon Coffee Shop. It's located on First Avenue, the main drag of the neighborhood. Which is mostly made up of the two huge hospitals, plus a whole bunch of nothing-special red brick, cookie-cutter apartment houses. The Parthenon has dark walls and weak lighting; never warm enough in the winter and torrid in the summer. And the smell! Essence of fried onions, steamed cabbage and hamburgers cooked in old grease.

But what's good about the Parthenon is it's halfway between my office and where I live, on 29th Street. What's bad about it is that every time I go there (which is a few times a day) I have to pass the County Psycho on the way. I've never been inside, but the place spooks me, even from the outside. Regular hospital buildings show a lot of activity – people walking in and out, windows open and lit up at night. This one is completely stumm, not a peep out of it, all the windows covered with mesh. Every time I walk by I listen for a cry – "Get me out of here, I'm not crazy" – or somebody trying to bust through the window so they can jump. It's as if the building itself is mentally disturbed, not just the poor suckers inside.

At the Parthenon, George and Theo – probably the owners under some complicated Greek arrangement – know what I want to eat even before I do. And here's another thing: Sometimes, late at night, after a bout with one of my kinky-haired social workers, with the blood rushing back to my stomach after an emergency bypass below, I get hungry and call up the Parthenon for a pizza. Could be Persian Pete serves something fancier, like champagne and caviar, to his dates after the main event. He'd have to, if he ever wanted to have another go at them; the jerk. Anyway, ten minutes later, on the button every time, Phil (real name Pheidippides, the night waiter at the Parthenon) rings the bell. Short and wiry, a spitting image of the pictures of the guys who kept running around with the flame in ancient Greece. I ask you, where else in New York City, except in some super fancy hotel, can a guy get 24-hour room service?

A good deal all around, except for one thing. The Parthenon has lousy bagels. They're all swollen-looking and pale; so soft you can sink your fingers into them. They have no taste whatsoever. When you bite into one, it's like trying to chew moist cotton. No use toasting them. That's when they look and taste like burned cardboard. Don't expect any help from the *schmier*, either.

I sit down in my usual booth, second from the door, with a direct southerly view down First Avenue. Customary bagel with cyclops eye staring at me, daring me not to eat it. Coffee, little plastic cup of creamer, and dispenser of artificial sweetener, all laid out for me like instruments in the OR.

For a couple of weeks, I was spending a lot of my time composing the little talk I'd just given at the conference. The patter modest enough on the outside. But to those in the know, a few well-placed fuckyous to people who shouldn't have lost faith in me in the first place. Still, by going public, I opened myself up to something else. People on the outside were sure to get hold of the little bit of information I'd come up with, and use it for their own purposes. That's the way it is in research. News spreads as fast as small-town gossip when the parson is caught exchanging confidential organ materials with the lady who plays the eponymous at the village church. Meaning I had to hurry up and figure out the electrical fire business.

Arson was always a possibility.

CHAPTER ELEVEN
RAT TIME

April 1984

So, I said to myself, how about if the locus ceruleus gets burned to the ground because a burst of electricity – an epileptic seizure – hits it head on, like lightning striking a house? That made a lot of sense. But, if it's a seizure that brings on all the damage, where does it come from, what makes it happen? Not to speak of how does a smoking, gutted locus ceruleus translate itself into a spur-of-the-moment suicide?

The way I began to figure it, we're all born with a suicide center, only it's equipped with a safety switch that is permanently in the "off" position. With almost everybody, the center has zero function all our lives, and dies the same time we do. But in some people – oftentimes blood relatives, which means they share some genes – there's an electrical storm, a seizure, in the center. In all the excitement, the safety switch gets unlocked. The countdown starts right then for the index finger to pull the trigger, for the legs to take their last ever jump.

There was only one way to show if this theory of mine wasn't just another pretty face. What I had to do was talk a suicide center into doing its specialty fire-swallowing act, then let the brain take care of the rest.

I still had some grant money for the Beethoven and Babe Ruth project. This meant I could cheat for a while, use the money to finance the suicide project instead. I knew there'd be hell to pay afterwards, when the Genius Foundation (no kidding, that's what it's called) found out I'd siphoned off their dough. Sort of like using the in-laws' wedding present to buy a diamond bracelet for the girl you're fucking on the side.

My lab was in the basement of the County. Not an elegant address, but enough out of the way to discourage drop-ins. I also had an office up on the neurosurgery floor of the hospital. That's where I worked at my official job, holding the hands of the trainees. The grimy halls and weak lighting in the basement made you feel you were walking into an old-time coal mine. Inside, not too bad. In a little anteroom, Marian, my long-time devoted lab assistant-receptionist, had her desk. It was also a waiting area, with a few chairs lined up against the wall. Most afternoons her four children sat there. Too young to go home after school, and the County doesn't pay enough to cover babysitters. The lab was good-sized, with an alcove up front that had plenty of room for the animal cages. That still left some space for the electrical equipment.

It didn't take long to get going, starting off on the cheap: a hundred high-grade white rats, plus some variable voltage electrical stimulators. I didn't even have to hire any extra personnel. Which was good, seeing as I didn't want too many people knowing what I was up to. Marian could feed the rats and serve as an extra pair of hands.. No worry there.

Rats have a locus ceruleus, same as humans. But whether they have a suicide center was up for grabs when I started the experiment. The idea was to zap one or the other locus with enough electricity to set up a seizure, then see what happens.

Over the next couple of months, I tried all kinds of combinations. So much and so much voltage to one locus or another – or both – for each rat. But what if I came in one morning and found one of the rats dead? How would I know if it was just a rat thing, or that it killed itself? The Genius Foundation had to come up with even more money, so I could buy a video system for 24-hour surveillance of the rats. For a while, that didn't pay off. They kept sitting around looking cheerful, eating up the feed, and not doing what they were supposed to do; namely, knock themselves off. I had to find a better way to spark the seizures.

Up in the OR, we'd been fiddling around with high-voltage lasers to loosen up scar tissue and stop the bleeding from tiny little vessels in the brain, the one you can't get at with a clamp. The discharge from a laser comes in focused bursts, not all at once. That way the area where the beam hits doesn't get damaged. Like staying in the hot sun all day long, versus ducking in and out of the shade. One'll get you a hell of a sunburn; the other, a nice tan.

Louie Rosenkrantz is in charge of lasers at the County. If you need one, or the one you have goes bad, he's your man. A balding beanpole in his thirties, he comes to work with a lunch pail, the kind little kids used to carry to school. Never left home, still lives with his mother. But when he's working with lasers, he's John Wayne and Einstein put together. I explained my problem to him and he came through like a champ. He made some changes in one of the lasers they used for eye surgery, and pretty soon I was in business. Not only did he lend me a machine, but he also pointed me in the right direction. Explained that the wavelength of the beam the laser sends out can be adjusted. He suggested I use different voltages and different wavelengths when I aimed the beam at the rats' heads.

Pretty soon I had to buy another two hundred rats. This voltage, that frequency, to the right or left focus. The bookkeeping alone, what I gave to each rat, took a couple of hours a day. Marian had to work overtime just to feed the rats, water them and clean the cages. If anything good was going to happen, now was the time.

One morning, we found one of the rats dead. Blood on his fur, and a broken neck. Buying the TV camera turned out to be a good investment. The tape showed everything that happened. During the night, he stayed quiet. Until, all of a sudden, he started running full force at the bars of the cage. Kept banging his head against them. To me, it looked a lot like the amateur suicides. No warning; then deadly violence aimed inwards. I pulled out the records and checked animal number, voltage, and wavelength, and whether it was the right or left locus. My notes showed four hundred volts with a wavelength of 3904 Angstroms. That measurement put it in the range of ultraviolet light. The locus? The right one, just like the amateur suicides we'd worked on at the ME!

You wait a long time for something to happen, and when it finally does, you're still surprised. Research has a way of biting you in the ass, so it's only beginners who make the mistake of getting excited too soon. The first thing I did was remove the rat's brain. No need for a big pizza sack. This time, a little Bloomies shopping bag was all I needed.

Murray came in for a lot of kidding from his staff when he scheduled an emergency MRI on the rat brain. Without waiting for the reading, as soon as Murray had finished, I rushed it over to the ME. Peter Bishop pretended it was a human brain I was bringing him; couldn't understand why it was so small. "Maybe the owner of this," his gloved right index finger pointing at the tiny brain lying before him, "visited a shrink just before dying?"

While Peter was dissecting and cutting the slices for the microscopic, I gave Murray a call to get the results of the MRI. He couldn't come to the phone, but the message he sent through the secretary, "you're right on the button," said it all. That meant the rat's right locus ceruleus must have had that peculiar mottled and gray look on the MRI, just like the amateur suicides. Much could still go wrong, but the message from Murray gave me a big lift. The MRI and the microscopics had gone hand-in-hand 100% of the time in the human suicides. So it stood to reason that it wouldn't be any different in the rat. Sure enough, when the slides came back, the rat's right locus showed the same destruction we'd seen in the ME cases. No question about it, that day's results brought me a lot closer to proving what I'd figured to begin with: that an electrical fire in the right locus ceruleus set up a chain of events which ended up as an inside job. No forced entry. The victim knew his killer. Himself.

I knew what I had to do next. Shoot the laser beam, four hundred volts and wavelength 3904 Angstroms, at the right locus of another fifty rats. Just to double-check what we found in the first one.

Now that I was so close to figuring out what makes the suicide center tick, I had to do something about Louie's laser. It was way too big, the size and weight of a sixteen-inch TV. Also, the probe, the business end that sends off the beam, was hard to maneuver. It had the heft of a Polish sausage. Wrestling with this cumbersome equipment and a squirming rat took up a lot of time. What I needed was a hand-held laser gun, like the ones they use to zap people in those intergalactic soap operas. I wanted the probe in place of the barrel, and the ultraviolet energy generated in what would be the handle of a conventional pistol. That way, I could hit whatever spot I was aiming at on the head of the rat from outside the cage, while it was sitting inside minding its own business.

Louie didn't say yes, and he didn't say no. He just said he'd get back to me. In the meantime, I continued the experiment with the fifty rats. No time off, except for some late-night sessions with my latest kinky-haired social worker, Eileen II, who always carried a camera around wherever she went. An old Rolleiflex, really small. It had to be, considering some of the nooks and crannies she got into before she shot off the flash. She took pictures before, during, and after. She picked out what she called "the best" and made a little album for me. Not the kind of collection you'd leave lying around on your coffee table...

I kept going to the weekly conferences, but didn't have much to say. Just about getting some data together, and that I'd be making a progress report soon. Meanwhile, my landlord kept threatening me, the jerk. He'd found a crack in the outside wall of the building, next to my windows. Claimed the weight of my books was making the place tilt. He was already after me on account of the bookworm misunderstanding. So now he had two reasons to *kvetch* about me at Housing Court.

Forty-eight of my rats did what I expected. They threw themselves against the bars, anywhere from a few days to a couple of weeks after getting hit with the laser. Also their MRIs and microscopics were exactly the same as the ones from the first rat and the amateur suicides from the ME; meaning I was right on the money in making the suicide center do its number. There were just two brains I couldn't use for my statistics. They were too damaged from the strength the rats used in throwing their heads against the bars. But you gotta admit, a 96% success rate is not exactly chopped liver.

But the experiment wasn't over yet. Now I had to make sure large animals did the same as my rats. Someday, I was going to make use of what I found out for the sake of people like Eva, innocent bystanders killed by a fire that went out of control. Learn to screen who's at risk and check out the genetics. Medicines against seizures, tailored to hit just this one center? Gene transfer therapy? As soon as I found the time, I was going to get back to the pure science.

I'd been leaving him messages, off and on, for a couple of weeks. No answer. But he finally showed up at my lab one afternoon, carrying a shoebox. He apologized for not coming up with the gun I asked him for. The batteries he needed to power the laser wouldn't fit into the grip. So he removed the guts of an old 35mm Nikon SLR – that's how he found room for the ultra-high intensity rechargeable batteries, and the machinery which translated their energy into a laser beam. He fitted the laser beam generator into where the telescopic lens usually sits, but kept the viewfinder and the inner lens. That way I could focus where I wanted the beam to hit. Now I was getting ready to do my final testing. On primates.

CHAPTER TWELVE
MY LINK WITH LYNX

May 1984

New York is full of bests. Best clowns for Upper East Side children's birthday parties. Best diners off the Long Island Expressway when you're coming home from the Hamptons. Best laundries that don't fade the monogram on your Turnbull and Asser custom-made shirts. So, doesn't it make sense that there's a best place right here for checking out the latest news of your favorite Nazi war criminals? What the Chalfin Family Documentation Center has to offer is something like those "Where Are They Now?" features on TV or in the papers. You get to see an old-time child actor turned Buddhist monk, or a 1968 campus revolutionary transformed into a stockbroker living on Park Avenue. Were the Nazis in question still around? And if so, were they comfortable and happy? If the answer to the first question is "no," case closed. They got what they deserved. OK, but what if we come up with a double "yes?" That's when it's fantasy time. "If I could only get my hands on…" You'd do what? Throw them – live of course – into their own ovens? Listen to them howl as the fire gives them the third degree? Or how about this: chop off their limbs one by one, and their dicks too (if they own one) for good measure? Then hang them head down, so whatever blood they have left keeps their brains supplied with the knowledge of the terrible thing that is happening to them? The very thought of it enough to trigger – again – the longing for revenge by the people who barely survived the camps. Also by the children they had afterwards; the ones who grew up in safety here, but keep on inhaling the secondary smoke from those far-away chimneys.

Imagine you're having one of those complicated, unpleasant dreams. As soon as you wake up, you try to remember who the actors were, figure out what it meant, wishing there was a way to record what you saw. That's what the CFDC does in real time. It's in the business of recording dreams, but with a twist: collecting all there is to know about mass waking nightmares in the years 1941 to 1945. Who lived, who died. Where and how. All those stories, attached for good to the ones who wrote, produced, and directed the torment.

Personally, I don't go for sanitized titles attached to grim affairs. For example: the sign they had over the main entrance to Auschwitz, "Arbeit Macht Frei" (Work Makes You Free). "Death Makes You Free" would have been more to the point. But still, in all fairness, what more appropriate name could they have given to this best registry of the worst? Sure, they might have hit you in the eye with something like "Auschwitz, Sobibor and Treblinka Inc." Couldn't have told it apart from one of those legal firms. "Mr Sobibor's line is busy. But Mr Treblinka's available. Can you hold?" Or how about "Nazi War Crimes Ltd."? No good either. In the US there are support groups for anything from former serial killers to individuals who fantasize about sex with birds. That would have drawn calls from Holocaust deniers, itching to join up.

My real beef is with cleaning up the camps and putting up monuments. Making sense out of events; the cheaper version of trying to explain them. So, what should they have done after the war? Simple. Leave the camps there as they found them. The slippery floors stained red by the bloody dysentery. In all the hurry of the last days, the half-burnt carcasses, the piled up skeletons. You can depend on the stink coming out of the shit and the decaying bodies for a good long time. Like a tornado that won't go away. Bring everybody there, all the ones on the losing side. Maybe even some of the winners. They're not blameless either for what happened here. Stick their noses in it. Bad dreams guaranteed for a long time to come. No sanitizing. Use it as vaccination.

The CFDC has its home in the Chalfin Building, a forty-story office tower located at Madison Avenue and 39th Street. It's the crown jewel of the Chalfin real estate empire.

The late Sol Chalfin, who started it all, was a Treblinka survivor who worked as a diamond cutter. He arrived here in 1945 and started small. Bought run-down tenements in Brooklyn and mortgaged them to the bone. Used the money to buy more, and, by 1960, he had enough to acquire his first Manhattan office building. The rest, everybody knows. More office buildings, and a few hotels. Also, a couple of high-rise condos on Madison that appear – if you're standing in the middle of Central Park – like wistful giraffes, peering over the old-time Fifth Avenue apartment houses in front of them.

Sol was pushed to found the CFDC by his Treblinka bunkmate, the writer and Nobel Prize winner Mordechai Lynx. The deal was, Sol would donate the space and put up the money, and Lynx would be in charge. Plenty of graduate students and PhDs in Modern European History to do the heavy lifting. Lynx's real job was to be Lynx; add his moral weight to the project. Also to keep Chalfin company at their daily *Konzentrationslager* memorial lunches in his penthouse office. Broth, with a few potato peelings swimming in it, served in dented cups.

I knew already you couldn't just walk into the CFDC like it's your neighborhood lending library. You'd think the place was Masada or something. All requests for information by appointment only. Responses by mail a few weeks later. No looking up the files (they still used index cards then) on your own. That's where my old pal Frank Lieberman came in. Best Upper East Side dermatologist in *Between Fifth&Park* magazine six years running. He spent the rest of his time drawing pictures of concentration camp scenes, featuring variations on emaciated figures wearing crowns of barbed wire around their skulls. Making his work a natural addition to the books that overflowed punctually, every year around the Jewish holidays, from Lynx's reservoir of KZ lore.

I explained to Frank that I was doing historical research on neurosurgeons involved in the Nazi doctor experiments. Could he fix that up with the CFDC for me? He did even better. Got me an appointment with Lynx himself, who was going to make the arrangements personally. Why was I seeing Lynx? Because he's a big hypochondriac. Any doctor he does a favor for, automatically gets a spot in his address book, in the remote case of an emergency.

The CFDC is located on the thirtieth floor of the Chalfin Building. The large anteroom is separated from the receptionist by shatterproof glass. I announced myself via a telephone on the wall, like in those old prison movies when it's visiting time. After my name was checked, a door clicked open, and I found myself in a large room filled with floor-to-ceiling cabinets and ladies wearing yellow name tags in the shape of five-pointed stars. That threw me. Why not tattoo their forearms too, while you're at it?

At the far end there was a door marked "M. Lynx. Private."

Another click, and I was on the stairs to the upper floor. Lynx wasn't there yet, so I had a chance to look around.

Low ceiling, not much light coming from the narrow little windows facing in every direction; like in those German blockhouses on the Normandy landing beaches. Plaques and pictures taking up all the wall space. Lynx used to be Lynksz. He changed his name because the engravers of the testimonials and prizes he kept collecting misspelled it every time. In a prominent spot, the Mr Holocaust award of the Long Beach, NY Council of Jewish Women. No year mentioned, so maybe the title was for life? A low bookcase nearby, with first editions of every one of his books. On top of it—propped up on a little ebony stand as if it was the Gutenberg Bible—his latest, *All Mountains Look Down on Valleys*. A sequel to the previous year's *All Valleys Look Up at Mountains*. They perished, Lynx publish.

In the middle of the room, there was a Parisian café table under a little umbrella with "Cinzano" plastered all over it. Several of those uncomfortable little green metal chairs surrounding it. In the corner, a dull brown double-decker bunk bed. No mattresses—just straw coming out every which way. A little plaque on one end, lettering faded. "Guaranteed Genuine WWII Concentration Camp bunk. Dedicated to Mr Mordechai Lynx. THE FRANKLIN MINT. 1964." Looked like what *Architectural Digest* would call an accent piece. Who knows? One of these days, "concentration camp" may be in as a design strategy. I can see the logo now: "The KZ Collection by Ralph Lauren." Naked light bulbs, custom-stained and tattered blankets. Couch fabrics made to look and feel like mildewed straw.

The wooden frame looked lonely, standing there all by itself. For these bunks to make a statement, they ought to be standing shoulder to shoulder with their fellows. Jails within jails. Each prisoner entitled to only the space his body takes up, exactly how much air he displaces.

I was trying out the bunk when Lynx came in. He motioned for me to sit in one of the café chairs instead. Wiry little guy, big head, grayish cowlick reaching down to his right eyebrow. He had good English, only it sounded Hungarian. Lynx looked straight at me, 100% attention, zero interest; reminded me of The Chief. Then he started on the spiel he must have ready for people who see his office for the first time. He pointed to the café table. "It's what I wrote my first articles on, when I came to Paris after the camps. A few of my friends from that time got together and bought it from the Café Bébert. You know, on the Boulevard Bonne Nouvelle." I didn't know, but that didn't stop him. He reached under the table and brought out a wooden rack. The kind cafés in Europe drape their newspapers on, so the customers don't walk off with them. This one had a long sheet of parchment attached to it. "Read what it says," urged Lynx, "there's an English translation if you need one." It looked – or at least tried to look – like a medieval document, on the order of a marriage contract between Henry VIII and one of his wives. Calligraphy of the kind that invites you to fancy Jewish weddings in Westchester. You know, "the honour of your company." Dig the British "u."

I did need the translation, which said: "To a great man, from his faithful friends." It probably sounded better in French.

All I could say was, "Wow, your friends must really love you." Meanwhile, I sneaked a peek at his shirt: pale blue, obviously custom-made. Something different about it. A big oval cutout of the sleeve over his right forearm, framed in red stitching, revealed his tattoo from Treblinka. He caught my glance right away. "The shirt comes from Hong Kong. The guy who slept in the bunk under Chalfin and me makes them. Sir Vivor, he calls the company."

Lynx nodded in the direction of the bunk in the corner. "That's where I think," he explained. "Where I write my books. The straw sticking into me. The best place for me to remember the past."

"Like Prou…" I began to say, before he interrupted.

"What did Proust know? That spoiled boy writing in his perfumed bed, with those padded walls around him, like in an insane asylum." An instance of petulance, in contrast to all the "forbearance" and "tolerance" that twinkled nonstop in the tributes leading up to his Nobel Prize.

"What everybody forgets is, he's not the only Jewish bedwriter. There's Kafka, too."

For a moment, I thought I heard "bedwetter." But then I realized that he wasn't talking about making pipi under the sheets. "Bedwriter" must have been a direct translation from the Hungarian.

"Kafka didn't work in bed," I replied. "He wrote at the family dining room table, except when his father yelled at him. Which was kind of often, for a guy in his thirties."

He was just about to reply – who knew how he was going to get out of this one – when there was a knock at the door.

CHAPTER THIRTEEN

ALISON

May 1984

In walks this tall, medium-blond *shikse* with an upswept hairdo. Neck strangely arched forward, a few strands of escaped hair falling down over it. Dressed like one of those female lawyers on TV. Dark blue suit, Gucci vs. Hermes scarf at the neck. Skirt dropping straight down like a waterfall, starting point what I estimated to be the northern end of the cleft of her ass. None of that tight half-moon effect favored by the muchachas on the subway. Obviously not part of the filing crew; no yellow star on her chest, the total surface of which I inspected rapidly, but thoroughly. Looking right at home, so I figured she must be some kind of VIP around here. Couldn't see a cross anywhere on her. Therefore probably not some religious zealot working for the Jews out of self-purification and/or flagellation. Another possibility: she's the local *shabbes goy*. That's a Christian who turns on the lights and puts a match to the oven for the orthodox on the Sabbath; jobs the latter are forbidden to do on their own. Why did that come to mind? Because it would make sense to have a righteous Gentile around, sympathetic as hell to the suffering in the Holocaust, but with a big plus. She wasn't—couldn't—be a mourner. We Jews can't turn off the tears. She could keep the paperwork dry.

As soon as Lynx saw her, I could swear his forelock got less droopy and edged further down, below his right eyebrow. Maybe that's the way he greeted the milkmaids when he was a boy growing up in Transylvania. "Permit me to present Miss Alison Hamilton. She's in charge of research and…"

Right away, I felt that familiar aching in my calves, same as when you're looking down from the top of a tall building. Rapture of the heights. Along with the urgent need to swallow this woman whole, breathe her in, talk to her for forty-eight hours straight. I knew the symptoms well; I'd had similar attacks in the past. Same response – must be a reflex, because it's too quick for an intellectual decision – just as soon as we met. Same lack of response also.

In most other situations, my penis is on the same wavelength as the rest of me. For sure with the social workers. That means it signs on for the duration. But for the type I'm talking about, like Alison Hamilton, nothing doing from the get-go. Like a traffic light stuck on red. My Penile Paradox. The more you want, the less you get. The more you ache, the less you quake. The more you yearn, the less you burn. Worse yet, it's not like your spleen or your pancreas isn't coming on board. Here is a crucial part of you that couldn't care less. Not just once or twice, but every time.

The heartache. Pushing and pulling, stretching and twirling. A tactful silence from the participant turned spectator across the bed. Let's face it – the penis is the fall guy for decisions that come from on high. If the brain says no, it helps like a *toiten bonkes* (trans.: a dead leech) to try to reason with, apply warm or cold compresses to, or shake some sense into it.

Believe me, I've tried to figure out why it's yes with some, no with others. Maybe it has to do with the overwhelming desire I feel right from the start. Everybody knows about sexual politics. Show weakness at the very beginning, you may never recoup. What better way to give up early than giving yourself the *coup de grâce* in the hard-on department?

My ongoing problem makes me yearn for a Republican penis. No interference accepted from big government, AKA the brain. All decisions made at the grassroots level on a case-by-case basis. That way, no dissension in the lower ranks when it's love at first sight. But regardless of what I wish for, my penis is a Democrat. Which means it's spooked every time by orders from higher up.

Lucky I have my social workers. With them, no anguish, no conflict.

CHAPTER FOURTEEN
THE ST MARTON FIVE

May 1984

Alison Hamilton was no lightweight. Lynx made sure to tell me about her PhD from Princeton, and her thesis on Austrian concentration camp guards published by Knopf. I'd gotten into the CFDC by the back door, pretending I was there to do research on the role of Nazi neurosurgeons in the death camps. I'd have to watch my step. This girl was going to be tough to fool.

I don't even remember saying goodbye to Lynx. Next thing I know, I'm following her out of his office. The stairwell was narrow, like a closet, so I got an undiluted whiff of her as we walked down the steps to the main floor. Mostly soap, shampoo, and the odor of toes wrapped in lotion meeting expensive leather. Good enough to bottle, like those sprays to make your car smell new. Only thing missing: a hint of the fragrance situation under her skirt. The Underskirt Factor.

She explained the layout to me as we walked along. The larger room with the floor-to-ceiling files held the records for the inmates of all the camps. Where they were deported from, approximate date of death, or when they got released. That was the main function of the center. To let people know – one way or the other – what happened to their friends or relatives. The perps' section was in an alcove almost as big as the main area. Everybody cross-indexed. By name, camp where they worked, profession ("J" for judges, "M" for medical doctors, etc.), where they came from. Some of them stayed close to home, made a cottage industry out of killing and torturing. The info on the victims was written down on little cards, but each of these guys had a whole folder. That's where you could find their pictures, court records, and current whereabouts.

Getting the records on the St Marton boys was a snap. I had to watch my step at the Chalfin outfit by keeping up the bullshit that I was doing research about human experiments done by Nazi neurosurgeons. Until the very last minute, I wasn't sure what I was hoping to find. There were times when I wanted them all already dead, their lives cut off around the same time as my father's. But most often, I wanted to do them in myself. Those fantasies I had as a kid – of punishing the people who had taken him away from me – were now pushing for, pardon the expression, a final solution.

From what I found out, five of the seven were still around. Wagner, the jailkeeper, had died of cancer in the late Forties. And Czemenecz, Weissensteiner's brother-in-law, was killed on the Russian front. Weissensteiner was the only one arrested after the war because of a complaint against him by the French occupation authorities. Something about atrocities against civilians while he was a captain in the Wehrmacht serving in France. But he didn't do any time at all. The records got lost, not enough evidence – the usual. After the war he went right back to managing his tavern. Now he was retired and living with his daughter in Wiener Neustadt (address supplied), a town near St Marton. The picture attached to his file didn't look anything like Tommy Byrnes or the Joker.

Cropped white hair, thin face, pissed-off look. I would have blown my cover if I'd asked to have the picture copied, so I just filched it. I also did the same with the photos of the others. No use shooting the beam at the wrong people because of mistaken ID.

I studied the files and took notes, like in school. I didn't speak much German, so the fewer questions I had to ask when I was actually there, the better. Strobl, Baumgartner, Kleinert, and Hochberger still lived in St Marton or just outside. At least I wouldn't have to wander all over Austria looking for them.

Strobl, the game warden, spent the war training attack dogs. For all I knew, some of his graduates might have been stationed in Auschwitz, at the end of the railroad line. He came home in 1945, and went back to his old job. Now he was retired and living in Forchtenstein, where he was a volunteer tour guide at the ancient Esterhazy fortress.

Baumgartner was still managing his sawmill. Deferred from army service because of "essential work," he spent the war making money and attending weekly drills of the Home Guard. Kleinert, the Gendarmerie chief, was in the military police, stationed in Romania. No record of having been involved in war crimes there. By now he was a lay brother in the local church. Hochberger, the butcher, was a cook in the Luftwaffe, stationed at an airfield in southern Germany. He now spent most of his days with his daughter, Anny, who ran the store. The rest of the time he hung around Weissensteiner's tavern.

Those were my five, sentenced to death in absentia. No long-winded legal process à la Nuremberg. No last-minute begging for mercy. No mitigating circumstances, "We were drunk, we thought the bullets were blanks, we never intended to kill your Papa. It was all a big mistake!" None of that. And the beauty of it? They were going to carry out the sentence of the court themselves. Who knows better than you what you've done and why you did it? To be liquidated by the one who understands you best: yourself?

At times, while I was cooking up this scheme, I'd ask myself if I wasn't just a big coward, killing these murderers on the sly. Instead of executing them outright, man-to-man and at the very last minute, giving them the word: "This is for Brenner, you miserable piece of shit." Their pupils getting wide as they realize the jig is up. You know, the John Wayne school of Jewish revenge. A school with a very poor attendance record over the centuries.

But at the end of the day, Machiavelli's Prince won out over the Duke. The heroic gesture was less likely to succeed than my subtle method of directing them to self-destruct. That kind of elegance is hard to beat. I was all for revenge, but I couldn't see myself doing the shooting or the stabbing. To do that, you have to at least accept the possibility of being stabbed or shot in return. Or getting caught, and becoming another jailbird, like my father.

The St Marton Five were just small-time hoods, content with daylight robbery and the occasional murder. Not even close to the grand vision of a mass killing mogul like Eichmann. They mostly faded back into the woodwork after the war. Paid their taxes, helped old ladies across the street. There were too many like them to punish; there would have been more people in jail than out. But now Weissensteiner & Co. had ended up out of luck. Knocked off somebody whose son figured out a new way to get even. They weren't going to die in their sleep.

Still, I couldn't help wondering, what's with these guys? Pull all that terrible stuff, and right away afterwards go back to being solid citizens. The average man on the street. Nothing to suggest the serial pervert or professional sadist about him. Doesn't even realize he's done anything wrong. Hannah Arendt called it the "banality of evil."

It's scary to have people who don't seem all that different from the rest of us go off the deep end. No black hats to tell us who's who. No telling when they're going to do it again, or what's going to set them off. No special qualifications needed. The anonymous sticking it to the no-matter-who.

A while ago, on one of my weekly visits to the Strand book store, I picked up a book from the Forties. It had an intriguing title: *The Anality of Evil*. A few words about the author, Sister Rivka Magdalena, on the flyleaf. Birth name: Sidonie Kohn. Converted to Catholicism as a teenager and later took vows as a Carmelite nun. She died tragically, after choking on a Communion wafer, at Easter-Passover 1951.

Was it just a coincidence? In 1963, Arendt adds one lousy letter, a "b," and she comes up with a whole new catchy theory about what made them do what they did. People reciting it like a Hail Mary ever since.

For Sister Rivka, the anus is a symbol, the receptacle for what's happened in the past. It's also the last stop, everybody out. Evil doesn't just pop up out of nowhere like a jack-in-the box. There's always a smoking gun somewhere, with a long story leading up to it. Bismarck, the Hanseatic League, the Weimar Republic. You name it, she throws it in there to make her point. I'm with her all the way so far, except for the fancy German history bit; that's where we part company. I'm for a simpler explanation. Go back a few hundred years. Start telling little kids there are some strange looking people around—many of them nasally disadvantaged—who, first chance they get, will drink their blood. Worse yet, when these

83

kids grow up, the same people are going to screw them out of their money, and make them look stupid besides. Multiply that by a few generations, the story snowballs. The descendants of the kids, they end up not knowing what to think. If these bad guys are so subhuman, why do they come off superhuman at the same time? Then, just at the right moment, somebody comes along who gets rid of their doubts for them. "These nose people are subhuman," he screams, "and besides, they're a pain in the ass. Get rid of them, and they'll never play with your head again." So that's what happened. End of story.

By the time I'd taken notes on the files and snagged the snapshots of the St Marton Five, I went to Alison's office on the main floor of the CFDC to say goodbye. Same odor situation as in the stairway to Lynx's office, plus a hint of a perfume that must have cost $100 an ounce. I waved my arms around a bit, hoping some of it would settle on me. The aching in my calves wasn't about to subside. That, and the fragrance, was sure to give me a restless night.

She didn't have much to say. Not even "see you later," which is 99% of the time dishonest, but better than the "bye" – not even "goodbye" – with which she dismissed me. But, like I've been telling myself ever since, it wasn't "see you never" either. My dilemma was this: how could I keep what I was doing secret and still show off to her? She was the expert on the Nazi diaspora, so it was going to take her about two minutes to find out about the wave of suicides. But figuring out what's going on is a whole other story. Besides, why should she suspect me? Nobody in that office had seen me look up "St Marton" instead of "Neurosurgeons." On the other hand, I wanted her to suspect me, even just a little bit. Not a bad pretext for seeing her again. That way I could at least get her attention. Which is the Penile Paradox talking. But when you're not playing with a full deck, shouldn't you just take anything you can get?

CHAPTER FIFTEEN

ÖSTERREICH

June 1984

With any other experiment, I would have gone on to monkeys, then baboons, to make sure that larger animals, closer to man, reacted the same as my rats. But why have some chirpy monkeys or a few pleasant baboons kill themselves if it wasn't absolutely necessary? The up-against-the-wall jailhouse boys were not only available, but expendable. And, if for some reason it didn't work out now, no hurry. I could always try later.

I didn't tell anybody about what I was about to do. Nobody. And when the job was done, I'd keep it to myself too. Not that I was afraid of getting caught. At least not in New York City. Try to extradite a Jewish guy, a doctor yet, who's knocked off some Nazis. You'd have three or four million out there, spread all over the runways at Kennedy. On the contrary – if it did ever get out – I'd be a big hero. With a wall full of plaques, like Lynx. The Judah Maccabee Award for Jewish Avenger of the Century. Also, the Pope John XXIII Medal for Jews Who Do Away With Gentiles Who Really Deserve It. But there's always a downside: sooner or later, people would figure out how I did it. Then, watch out! A whole revolution in the way people murder each other. The gun industry in a major swoon. Maybe even a hiccough or major belch in the legal system. Are you guilty of homicide if you just induce somebody to commit suicide? Defendants with arguments like, "I was idly playing around with my laser. Next thing you know, my rich uncle, who was threatening to cut me out of his will, killed himself." All the way to the Supreme Court. Besides, I got to like the idea of being the Lone Ranger. Not good old Max; smart all right, but what a nerd! Instead, the new, unaccountable, mysterious me.

My victims are sure to keep in touch. If they don't know where it's all coming from, this wave of suicides, that's got to add an extra dimension of worry to their nights and days.

But anybody who cuts people's heads open for a living will tell you the same: no way you can figure out everything up front. It happens all the time: you pull a long face, tell the patient's relatives you're sure to find a tumor when you get in there. Come out of the OR, so happy to be wrong. It's a cyst, everything's going to be fine. It goes the other way too. Tell them it looks like a little blood pocket on the x-ray. When you find out it's really a cancer chock-full of blood vessels, you drag around as long as possible after the surgery, just so you don't have to tell them the bad news. Regardless of whether you spend six hours or six days getting ready, once in a while you'll get faked out, regardless.

When I got off the plane in Vienna, I'd spent so much time on the suicide project and on the logistics of how to knock off the St Marton Five, that I never realized how I would feel about setting foot in Austria. I was in the mindset of Max, the cold-blooded killer. Taking my cue from the likes of Alan Ladd. Did he check out the emotional temperature of a place he got sent to, to put his stamp on a contract? No way. But the minute I hit the line at passport control, any notion I might have had about modeling myself on that worthy flew out the window. The men checking the passports were still wearing those grey helmets with shiny black visors front and back, like in the old days. Also, the stamps coming down hard on the documents sounded to me like cell doors clanking shut. That made me remember how terrified my folks were when they hit the final checkpoint at the Swiss border. Erich checking his pockets every thirty seconds, making sure he still had those priceless exit permits. What if the Nazi authorities changed the rules and the permits weren't valid anymore? They'd be marched over to the next train heading back to Vienna. That was why I kept reaching into my pocket for my own passport, with "United States of America" stamped all over it.

Meeting up with the guy at the counter turned out to be a breeze. He stamped what he had to stamp, gave me a big smile, wished me a pleasant day; didn't ask me to produce my yellow star, or drop my pants. I came out of the main terminal feeling flat. I'd been in Austria for maybe an hour. I'd even met up with an official with vaguely Nazi headgear. Still, nobody had called me a dirty Jew yet. Not that I considered it a prerequisite, but it would have been helpful. An epicure comes to Paris and finds the restaurants closed. A cigar lover walks around Havana all day long and nobody's smoking. It was discouraging.

CHAPTER SIXTEEN

TROPIC OF CANCER

June 1984

Thought I'd attract too much attention if I spent a few days at a time in St Marton or one of the other towns nearby in Burgenland, the easternmost province of Austria. The locals might wonder what a foreigner was doing there. Or maybe not.

> Q: How many Burgenland electricians does it take to screw in a lightbulb?
>
> A: Two. One to test the socket; the other to notify his family.

Seemed to me it was safer to show up now and then, carrying what looked like a couple of fancy cameras. One, the real thing, meant to snap some of the sights around town. The other, a decoy containing the laser. Nothing lifelike about what it was designed to shoot.

That's how I ended up at Aunt Florence's. Not my real aunt. She and her husband, Uncle Emil, weren't relations, just old friends of the family. He'd come to the US in 1938. The Nazis had taken away his factories, and he didn't go back to running them until after the war. I must have been around fourteen when my parents took me along for a visit to their house in Greenwich Village. Aunt Florence turned out to be a bombshell in her late twenties.

Tall, with a peek-a-boo, Lauren-Bacall-type hairdo. Kind of a long face, like you sometimes see on Jewish females. Black skirt down to her ankles, and a man-style white button down shirt. A string of pearls meandered down from her neck, then disappeared through a trapdoor in the shirt. I have no recollection of what she smelled like. Sniffing women, to get an inside tipoff to what they're all about, comes later.

Up to then, I'd only been acquainted with what you could call the "utilitarian" type. My mother, my teachers in school, the ladies who attended temple. Dressed for the weather, sensible shoes, hairstyles right out of *Good Housekeeping*. Here, I was like a farm boy who meets up with a racehorse for the first time. Who never imagined the ones who pull the plows back home have city cousins like this. She could have been a shoo-in for the Penile Paradox roster. Not all that different from the others who've met the requirements over the years. Overwhelming stimulus smothering any possible response. But then, at that stage of my non-development, the Penile Paradox hadn't emerged yet. All I could do was store my first memory of her until later that day.

I was the only teenager in the place, and we ran out of conversation almost immediately, the adults and me. That was when I made a beeline for Aunt Florence and Uncle Emil's stuffed-to-the-limit bookshelves. That afternoon made up for all the times I had to make do with my parents' friends' *Reader's Digest* collections, or memoirs about the Zionist movement in the 1920s. *Tropic of Cancer* was a book that caught my eye right away, because of its familiar title. I was surprised at how thick it was, considering there were only a couple of paragraphs about the subject in our geography textbook. I began leafing through it, in case there was more to the subject than they were teaching us in school. I turned the pages, but there was nothing to do with geography that I could find.

I'll never understand that title. Otherwise, no complaints. More fun than maps, and a lot less dry. The one who's telling the story, Henry Miller, goes on and on about his friend Maxie's sister. Not so much about her, but about her quim. I'd never heard the word before; not since either. A lot of the expressions were completely foreign to me. Words like "orgasm," and "erection." Also, if I remember right, "back-scuttle" and "twat."

At this point, I hid the book under my shirt and slunk off to the bathroom. You try to look casual, while you're making for the john with a big bulge sticking out of your belly. Like POW's masquerading as locals in those WWII escape movies.

I wasn't totally ignorant in these matters, just completely. I had carefully examined a few drawings that came across my desk in school. Sent around the classroom via a kind of bush telegraph. Mostly, two figures with a thin rectangle hooking up their middles, like a bridge. Other times, the rectangle went from the middle of one into what looked like the head of the other. Contrary to the old adage, one word in Miller's geography lesson was worth a thousand pictures. I'll never forget that afternoon. Meeting Aunt Florence, for starters. Also finding out from Henry – by now we were on a first-name basis, considering he was so ready to come clean with a new reader like me – about the various possibilities hopefully awaiting me. In imitation of Henry, who did it to – and had it done to him by – Rita, the proprietress of the quim, in the vestibule of her house in Brooklyn.

I'd stayed in touch with Aunt Florence off and on. So now, when I wrote to her that I was coming to Vienna, she invited me to stay at their house. By now she must have been in her early fifties, and was only what you'd call "handsome." Face still long, a nonspecific hairdo this time around (Lauren Bacall, where have you gone?) dressed mostly in woolen skirts, sweaters, and hiking shoes. Like an Austrian *Hausfrau* who's ready to climb a mountain any minute. Not much left of the glamorpuss look that made me so nuts a long time before.

What I'd been planning to do was rent a car and take trips down to where the St Marton Five were patiently waiting to be subjects in my experiment. I calculated it would take from a few days to a couple of weeks for the laser beam to do its job. At least, that's how long it took with my rats. When (I wasn't about to think if) my potential victims killed themselves, that was sure to hit the papers. Especially if they did it at random, one after another.

I told Aunt Florence I was going to take some day drives outside Vienna. Check out the country my parents came from. She looked all excited when I mentioned what I had in mind, volunteered to drive me around, why did I have to rent a car? Wouldn't I like some company? That's all I needed, I thought to myself; a kibitzer for my revenge scenario.

She almost pleaded to come along. That long-ago Sunday afternoon, if she'd just offered to show me the way to the bathroom, I would have kissed every pearl of her necklace, especially after it disappeared down the trapdoor. Followed by a nocturnal emission in the daytime.

"No, thanks," I said. "I usually do my best traveling on my own. It might be hit-or-miss, but I prefer it to a guided tour." All that bullshit. "But in the mornings, could we do some German lessons?" I said I'd heard translating newspapers works best. Didn't tell her what I really had in mind; that continuing the same lessons over the phone, when I was back in New York, would keep me up to date about the latest undoings of the St Marton Five.

CHAPTER SEVENTEEN
ST MARTON

June 1984

The day after my arrival, I made straight for St Marton. By now, I was itching to see the place I'd only dreamt about. Whenever I'd tried to imagine it, the lighting was obscure; a sad town, darker than the surrounding countryside. It was like my mind was wearing sunglasses. Would the remnants of the dynamited temple be sticking out of the ground like a sore that refuses to heal, no matter how long it's been festering? And what about the Judengasse? Was there anything left of the old ghetto?

Coming from the east, the Vienna side, you roll down a steep hill with a church, and a long, low building that looks like a monastery, on the left. According to my mother, the Judengasse was the street you came to once you reached the bottom. No ruins to be seen there. What I saw instead was a pedestrian mall, with stores on either side. It could easily have been Paramus, on Route 4, only they were playing their own brand of elevator music. Lots of oom-pa-pa and marching songs.

I'd brought a photo with me that had hung on our living room wall as far back as I could remember. A picture of the Judengasse, the way it looked in the Thirties. You could see a group of four or five people in the foreground, with houses behind them. Also the temple, on the far left, where the street takes off from the square below the church. Erich attached names to the faces for me. Putzl, the *Dorftrottel* – village idiot – wearing thick glasses and a silly grin. Tibi Steiner, the owner of the shoe store, with a visored cap and a pipe in his mouth. A couple of kids wearing *yarmulkes*, the Rabbi's sons. Nussbaum the grain dealer, in a long coat and soft hat. The picture was just a reminder. So I could get an idea of what had been where, before they blew up the houses and got rid of everybody who lived in them.

First thing I did was walk over to where the temple used to be. You'd think it would leave some vestige of its existence, just some little artefact that managed to escape the destruction. Nothing doing. There was a Konsum supermarket in its place. I looked around for a plaque; maybe in front where they keep the shopping carts. The inscription on the order of "Here we feed the hungry, in the place where sustenance was so long given to the soul." Some ecumenical bullshit like that. Fahgedaboudit. You seen one four-hundred-year old temple, you seen 'em all.

A couple of doors down, there was an ice cream parlor with tables set out in front, under a canopy. There was a big sign that said "Sundaes," with pictures of various combinations pasted up all over the place. One of them grabbed me. Three scoops, different flavors, whole strawberries and a gob of whipped cream covering everything like a cloud. Plus, a little Stars and Stripes stuck on top. Anywhere else in the world, if only because of the flag, I'd have eaten the whole thing. But in this place, with the oom-pa-pa blaring, and the destroyed temple next door hovering over the scene, I couldn't. Doing it would have meant I'd gone along with what they had done. Torn the Judengasse out of the picture, and put up this country bumpkin Disneyland instead. Courtesy of the people I came here to hunt down.

Next, I went to look for the jail. According to my mother, it was a couple of hundred feet from the main square. I walked around and around, but couldn't see anything that looked like a jail. I didn't even care about finding the building, I was willing to settle for less. I needed to put my cheek against the wall that propped my father's head up when he died. Never mind the exact spot. Just to be able to touch the stone would be enough.

After a while, I came upon a plaque fixed to the gate of a little park. Only one word, "Gefängniss," looked vaguely familiar. Some dates underneath. 1892-1952. It's not often they get rid of a jail; usually it's the prisoners who take the hit. I walked into the park and sat on a little bench. For the first time ever, I was in a place where my father had already been. I had no idea where they buried him. Somewhere underneath where I was sitting? Could they have dug a hole in the ground, dumped him in there, and made everything level again? The same way they used to bury criminals, so the locals could walk all over what was left of them. At least in the early days in Dachau – when they were still killing one at a time – little canisters filled with ashes were delivered to their relatives. Who knew if the remains were the real article? They could have been somebody else's, or even sand. At least the ones left behind had something to hold onto.

Coming out of the park, I saw the irony of it. The St Marton Five were my main – actually my only – solid connection with what happened in there. Too bad they weren't going to be around long enough to tell me some stories about the old days.

To make me look like a harmless tourist, I even took some shots with the Nikon SLR. A couple of fountains, City Hall, the Emperor Franz Josef memorial. The decoy slung over the other shoulder.

Waiting.

CHAPTER EIGHTEEN

AUNT FLORENCE IN CHARGE

Late June, 1984

From working with my rats, I knew it took between seven and fourteen days, door to door, between the shot from the laser and the actual suicide. The Chief had only – reluctantly – given me a week off. So I knew from the get-go that I'd have to go back to New York and wait it out. Not that I didn't have a lot to think about anyway. Most of the amateurs I met up with at the ME, and Eva too, went out with a bang. Hanging from a hook, jumping off a bridge, swallowing rat poison; that kind of aggressive way of getting rid of themselves. But their right locus ceruleus had started burning on its own. "Directed" suicide – where I supplied the electricity that started the fire – could have a different effect. My St Marton rats could end it like a bunch of pussies; sniff at the gas range, or take a few pills. Not enough to do any real harm. Or go berserk. No way to know.

My agenda was simple enough. Figured on spending part of the day killing my Nazis, and the rest of the time being squired around Vienna by my once-sexy aunt. Not forgetting about the language lessons either.

The first morning of my visit, I smelled coffee as soon as I opened the door to the hall. When I walked into the breakfast room, there was Uncle Emil, sporting a forest green jacket with epaulets, and matching pants. All decked out, like for a hunt. I haven't said much about him. Trouble was, the rare times I saw him when I was a kid, he'd only talk to my folks. Me, he treated like a pet dog they'd brought along. This time around, we had a different problem. He kept calling me Erich, and followed me around all the time, speaking Hungarian.

I asked him where he was going, that it must be some important event. But he was just going to see his buddies at the Emperor Franz Josef club, a high-class daytime nursery for senior citizens. Before leaving, he added a Tyrolean hat, complete with a yellow feather stuck in the band. He looked pretty snazzy, except I began to wonder about the feather. Could it have the same significance as the long-ago yellow star? In case the good old Nazi days come back and it's open season again for spitting in faces and taking target practice on certain chosen people?

Aunt Florence was wearing a *schmatte*, a nondescript housedress favored by Jewish ladies when they're about to tackle a long overdue cleaning of the toilet bowls. But as soon as the door slammed on Uncle Emil, she excused herself. Came back a few minutes later in a long silk gown with a little fur collar, a peignoir, and that same disappearing-down-her-front string of pearls she had on the first time I ever met her. It still made me wonder about its final destination.

I felt underdressed. Read somewhere that Vienna etiquette dictates that male houseguests wear pajamas for breakfast. I don't own any of those, for the simple reason I've slept in a scrub suit ever since I was in training. In the hospital, it's the right outfit for every occasion. The OR, the cafeteria, chatting up a student nurse at the door to some remote linen closet – wherever. And of course, for falling into, or jumping out of bed, without having to perform some complicated toilette while you're half asleep. Scrub suits do have one disadvantage, though; they don't come with a fly front. Meaning, if you want to liberate something, you have to first untie the string at the top, and pull down the pants. Usually not a problem, except if you need to present the something in a big hurry.

Aunt Florence was being the charming hostess. She'd sent Uncle Emil out to the bakery earlier, so I could have still-hot poppy seed rolls to go with my English tea. Also, there were a half a dozen newspapers sitting on a little pile next to her, along with some yellow pads, pencils and a German-English dictionary. Just as soon as she cleared the breakfast dishes, we'd be starting the first lesson.

By now, it was way too late to be learning German. When I was a kid, it would have been way more useful to speak the language. My parents would be speaking English, when, all of a sudden, like when you twirl the dial on a shortwave radio, they switched languages. That's what happened when my mother's friend Barbara went missing during a vacation in the Catskills. She came back a week later, claiming she'd lost her memory. My mother and Erich laughing and exchanging sly looks. Except I was tuned out, which pissed me off. That time, I wished the war was still on. I could have called the FBI to turn in my parents, who I'd heard discussing a mountain range near New York City, in the tongue of the enemy.

First off, Aunt Florence showed me the newspapers. Wiener this, Wiener that. For obvious reasons, I needed the St Marton paper to be in the mix. I'd need the news from there some day very soon.

Aunt Florence was a teacher before she hooked up with Uncle Emil. No wonder the first lesson started out so well. Show and tell, repetition, question and answer. That went on for about an hour. I should have realized something was up, the way her face got more and more red. Maybe it's the heat, I thought, with that fur collar making it worse. And/or change of life. Suddenly, didn't see how it happened, one of the newspapers came floating off the dining room table. I hate when that happens. It's a bitch to put a newspaper back together after it's come apart. It was obviously up to me to crawl under the table and set things right. Which I started to do.

I was just getting on my knees when, next thing I knew, Aunt Florence was on my back. Not about the lesson. Literally. Jamming my face into the front page I was just picking up in the process. "What kind of a girl do you take me for?" I wanted to cry. Pleasantly chatting one minute, nailed to the floor the next. I didn't know what to do. This much was obvious: sooner or later, I'd have to turn around and face the music those pearls were making, clack-clack, on my thoracic spine. People who are about to drown see their lives flashing by in an instant. With me, it was the immediate future and the possible long-range effects, if I gave in.

Harboring a hard-on in scrub pants is no walk in the park. Very little give in the material. What you see is what there is. I mean, if you want to send a message to the person it's dedicated to, all well and good. But if you're trying to hide it, that's where it gets to be a problem. So – once I turned over – there was no way I could claim I wasn't interested. But in what direction was this erection leading me?

Meanwhile, no escaping the sound of the rustling of the peignoir and the whooshing of the fur collar. "Just listen to Mama, baby, and everything's going to be swell," Aunt Florence announced.

For a brief moment, I was hoping it was all a big mistake. That she had had an urgent message from my mother, and she chose to tell it to me lying down. Ruled that possibility out right away, seeing as it was 4am in New York and my mother was by then in a nursing home, the administration of which was sure to frown on their gaga patients making middle-of-the-night transatlantic calls. What Aunt Florence was murmuring in my ear brought all my doubts to a head, which were much too important to just sweep under the rug. And not only because all my weight was on it, which made any whisking physically unlikely. Anyway, here was my problem the way I saw it.

You know already Aunt Florence is not my real aunt. With her, the title is just an honorific. The same way they used to call the bordello piano virtuoso in the old days "Professor." When I was growing up, attaching "Aunt" or "Uncle" to the names of family friends showed both respect and familiarity. But even if she was just an honorary relative, Aunt Florence being an old friend of my mother's brought up a very sensitive issue: the incest taboo. With her I didn't even have the Penile Paradox to help me out.

That was pretty clear if you looked at things from the viewpoint of my scrub pants. Turned out I'd somehow escaped it with Aunt Florence. First time around, it was all in the abstract anyway; I was too young when I met her. After that, I didn't see her for many years, by which time the bloom was off her particular rose. In other words, she was already on the downslope from over the hill. Let's face it, I was in a big-time state of conflicted feelings.

By now, the pearls were really digging into my back. Even just considering the pain, I knew the jig was up. Something had to be done -- pronto. I flipped right over on my back. No use fighting history. Many men over the years must have faced similar choices. Here, the decision was taken out of my hands. I've already told you: my penis leans to the Left; politically, that is. But in Aunt Florence's case, it switched parties, voted Republican. Result: the grassroots revolution inside my scrub pants.

But the moment I turned around, I thought of what I was

going to call her, now that our relationship had taken this sudden U-turn? Let's say we're in some transport of passion. What do I say? "Aunt Florence, could you shift around so I can slip…?" Or the other extreme, "Hey bitch, turn over so I can…?" There's always the respect factor to consider. Just because the give and take between the two of you has moved its place of business a couple of feet down from where it used to be, and the status is never going to be quo again, doesn't mean there's any excuse for bad behavior. I quickly made up my mind. From now on, I was going to call her "Flo."

She was all business from the very beginning. My way or the highway. That was the start of my career as a Vienna Toyboy. "Toyman" would have been more to the point, since I was already in my early forties, and an academic neurosurgeon with a professorship in my future. Sounds kind of stuffy though, so "Toyboy" it had to be. "Do this, do that," "turn your head a little bit," or "open your mouth wider." Anybody would think they'd stumbled into a dentist's office.

My career as a sex object had officially begun, and there was no let-up as long as I stayed in her house. A fixed routine. I always found it painful to meet up with Uncle Emil in the mornings. That he thought I was my stepfather, and a Hungarian speaker at that, only added to my guilt. As soon as I heard the door slam, I got out of the scrub pants, because working the string made her cranky. First, breakfast. You'd be amazed at the sensual effect of poppy seeds in free fall, raining down on an unprotected crotch. Then sixty minutes, exact, reading the papers, learning the language of my ancestors.

I don't want to give you the impression I was some kind of a victim, forced into things against my will. It's true she was in charge all the way, but I sure as hell loved what my captor was doing to me. I can't even say we got a lot closer, that all that sex ended up as a full-scale affair. No romantic dinners on the banks of the Danube, the gypsy orchestra playing for just the two of us, as we danced one last waltz, with the sun starting to peep around the edge of the Iron Curtain. Wild thoughts about a future together, come what may. None of that stuff. She never once asked me about what I do, what my life is all about. Never opened up about herself. So that's the way it stayed between us. I was her sex object. Every day, right on schedule, she accidentally on purpose dropped one of the newspapers. That was the signal for my decentralized penis to rise and shine. Pure reflex. Under the table, with carpet burns developing on my knees and elbows, I once asked whether we couldn't move to a more skin-friendly environment. No answer. All she did was dig in harder. She had the home-field advantage.

Still, there's no denying it, Aunt Florence turned out to be a handful. She let me know right away that her button system was my responsibility. That if things didn't work out under the piano, it was my fault.

I'd already learned about the button setup, courtesy of my frizzy-haired social workers. It's located in the area just south of the pubic bone, on both sides at the top of a woman's velvet underground. Something like what's on the instrument panel of an airplane for starting the motors, switching fuel tanks, techno details like that. Just as with different makes of planes, no two women are wired the same way. You push what looks like the identical button, but there's no predicting what effect it's going to have. You have to keep experimenting until you get the connection straight in your mind. That can take a good long while, with everybody exhausted at the end. And it's not even as if she can make it much easier for you. Having never been there – made eye contact – she can only point in the general direction. After that, it's still hit or miss.

More often than not, the right side is a booby trap. Three buttons, going from bad to worse. Once, I accidentally hit the one that brought on Aunt Florence's pubocranial reflex. Right away she got a splitting headache, which put her out of commission for a while.

After that, I stayed away from that side altogether. For good reason. The other two buttons had been a lot of trouble for me in the past. With Eileen I, to be exact. When I pushed on one, all of a sudden she wasn't sure she wanted to do it with a man anymore. Got all philosophical about how she'd be better off having her mind penetrated, instead of her body, by somebody with basic equipment similar to her own. Just idly brushing by the last one on the right, I was in instant deep shit. She couldn't stop vomiting, supposedly because she couldn't stand the smell of my deodorant. At the same time, there was a short circuit, which made the whole button system go dead. It took a while for the lights to go back on again.

I had much better results with Aunt Florence when I stuck to the left side. Here, three of the buttons are spread out every which way, but – and here's the hitch – only one works. The other two are dummies, not connected to anything. Push on them all night, all you get is a cramp in your hand. The Real McCoy, I call the O Button. Not easy to find, hidden behind a little curtain most of the time. But draw the curtain aside, watch out! At least, that's what I was given to understand by Aunt Florence's pearls clacking away, even though their owner was lying perfectly still.

I know the postcoital (just a generic term; no use going

into specifics) cigarette has its own niche in the history of love. Personally, I prefer the postcoital lunch. Relaxed. Civilized. Good table manners making all the other manners good too. Every day, after we got out from under the table, I took a shower, got dressed in regular clothes and shared a lunch of ham, sausages, sauerkraut, and a couple of bottles of beer with Aunt Florence. By then, she was all spiffed up, looking more like her old self. None of the I'm-about-to-climb-a-mountain outfit she'd worn on my arrival. Silk pants, a tailored blouse, and those pearls. No peignoir this time, but she had a look about her which suggested she was ready to start all over again. No go. I only had a week to do in the St Marton Five. The afternoons were reserved for beaming my laser.

Besides, even when I was in my twenties, one session a day was plenty for me. Maybe not even that often, considering I'm in an irregular line of work. Doing what I do is not like being a writer or a painter. They can discharge whatever they've got left after they write maybe a hundred words, or draw a couple of lines. Also, they can do it as often as they want, since they're self-employed. It's supposed to give them inspiration, from what I hear. I could just see myself taking a break between operations, in some unisex locker room. There, I could spritz my creative juices all over my girlfriend, with the result that I could approach my next case – let's say an about-to-pop blood vessel – with a purer artistic vision.

At the beginning, I figured the morning session under the table would do the job for the whole day. I always got a kick out of it, but I also found it stressful. Same as assisting The Chief in the OR. You always find yourself working out in advance what he expects you to do. I've had my hand spanked too many times, always with the heaviest instrument handy. Takes something out of you, trying to stay out of trouble.

CHAPTER NINETEEN

EXPERIMENTING WITH PRIMATES

Late June, 1984

I was going to do the four local boys first, keep Weissensteiner for dessert. The decoy SLR was ready to roll, all charged, courtesy of the transformer I brought along to convert the current to two hundred twenty volts, which is what they use in Austria. Louie Rosenkrantz, my unsuspecting accomplice, left the viewfinder in the camera when he took out the part that takes the pictures. That way, I could focus exactly where I wanted to shoot the laser beam. On the rats, I'd found out the best place to hit was a spot behind the right ear. That was where my human subjects were going to get it too. No reason why I shouldn't hit the right locus ceruleus straight on, like I always did; I'd had a lot of practice by then. Tickle the spot in the suicide center where it likes to be tickled. The rats did it. So could a few Nazi primates.

The first day, I was just getting oriented when I spotted him. Hochberger, the butcher turned cook for the Luftwaffe, sitting on a bench outside his old store. He didn't look all that changed from the picture I was carrying around with me. Narrow little eyes, round, reddish face. Short-brimmed hat, a feather sticking out of it, on top of his head; a cane propped up next to him. I could see a woman behind the counter, serving customers. Figured it was his daughter Anny, according to the CFDC info.

He looked like he was just starting to doze off. That meant he wasn't going to be moving much, which would make my job easy. There was a fresco, two angels juggling another one – or vice-versa – over the entrance to the building. I made a big show of focusing on the fresco, and only at the last second moved the focus down and over a little bit, until I had old Hochberger in the picture. From about twenty feet out, I shot the laser at the right side of his head, just behind the ear. No muss, no fuss. Just the usual little clicking and hissing sound. Different, but not too different, from what you hear when somebody takes a picture with a fancy camera. I detected a faint smell of something burning. But on the street, who was going to notice?

As soon as I'd pulled the trigger, and closed the camera, I felt let down. *Post coitum omne animal triste.* No big surprise. I'd been working my way towards this moment most of my life. If I had killed Hochberger outright, for sure I would have felt an instant sense of catharsis, of release. But here it was more like I swallowed a cathartic. Your insides take their own sweet time when you ask them to do a job for you. I'd just have to wait it out.

After moping around for a while, I started looking at the bright side, thinking about what I'd already pulled off. And there was more to come. This was just the beginning.

That night, I kept shuffling their pictures in front of me, the ones I'd filched from the CFDC. Hochberger had been unexpectedly easy. Snoring away, presenting his best profile to me. No way I could have missed. Still, twenty feet was the outermost range of the laser beam. That's why I needed to get close enough, without getting a lot of attention from my target or anybody else nearby. Louie Rosenkrantz had looked at me funny when I asked him to give me as much distance as he could. Was I getting lazy, he wanted to know, maybe thinking of shooting the rats from home? Ha-ha. He never did give me a long distance lens.

Each of the perps was going to be a different kind of photo opportunity. They didn't need to be napping, they didn't need to hold still and look at the birdie. The release time of the laser was extra short, like a very fast shutter speed on a real camera. Once I focused, all it took was a few milliseconds to hit the mark. IF I got close enough.

I had the pictures laid out on a fancy-looking table in my room in Aunt Florence's apartment. Biedermeier, as she had instantly informed me, from the nineteenth century. I wasn't sure if it was to keep me from scratching it up, or she was just putting on airs. You know, that special look Jewish girls get–the end of the nose turned up and leaning slightly sideways, eyes narrowed–when they're discussing antiques. Conveniently forgetting the closest they ever came to those while they were growing up, was what, Bronx Renaissance? I'd like to try to pull that in my apartment. "Ikea, you know, late twentieth century."

As I was laying out the pictures, I began seeing red. Four out of the five, including Hochberger, had a windburned look. Everybody but Weissensteiner, the only paleface among them. Looking like he'd spent his entire life in a dungeon as his primary residence.

Ever see the History Channel catch-ups with retired generals, chatting away about WWII, as if it was some long-ago World Cup? Funny thing is, the ones on our side all look like they're ready to kick the bucket any minute. White hairs sticking out of noses and ears, mismatched clothes, chins resting on their canes to keep from tipping over. The makeup is no help, only gives them an embalmed look. The ones from the other side? About the same vintage. They look like they could still be bellowing out orders in their fortified bunkers. Losing the war must be some kind of elixir of youth. Sitting straight up, with those little pins (what the hell are they anyway, to me they always look like born-again swastikas) stuck in their well-cut lapels. How they love to talk shop with their old-time opposite numbers. Pincers this, reserve divisions and pullbacks that. But what always gets me is their faces. Ruddy; like after skiing, with a couple of glasses of Glühwein thrown in. Looking not so different from my four out of five. That led me to wonder about the color coordination. If it was just from spending a lot of time outdoors, then the concentration campers who were kept at attention in the freezing cold for ten hours at a time should have died with rosy cheeks. Not the life-faking-death look the few that were left sported when the gates finally opened up – outwards. Then again, maybe it's heredity – my perps and their Wehrmacht officer soulmates sharing some innocent genetic fancy for a flushed kisser?

Hochberger I'd already taken care of, so that left Strobl, Kleinert, and Baumgartner in the immediate neighborhood. Figured I'd drop the Candid Camera bit for a day in St Marton, and move up the road a few miles, to Forchtenstein. That's where the ancient Esterhazy fortress sits on top of a low-rising mountain. The ideal place to zap Strobl, ex-game warden and wartime attack-dog professor. I'd known about the place since I was little. Erich, my number two father, would tell me stories about the well in the main courtyard. A certain Duke had a lot of wives, one after another. He traded them in on a regular basis, like last year's Cadillac. A guy with commitment phobia, it sounds like. What he did was throw these ladies down that deep well, whenever he felt the need for a change of scenery in his bedroom. Serial monogamy, Austrian style. Scared the shit out of me. Every time I heard about those amphibious wives, I thought that it could easily happen to a kid like me, if I didn't toe the line. That the well was a few thousand miles away from Fort Lee, New Jersey reassured me during waking hours. But go tell that to your dreams. I'd been toilet-trained for years (Austrian parents frown on the walking wet) by the time Erich began to tell me this bedtime story. Every time he did, I had a nightmare as soon as I fell asleep. I was floating in water, at the end of a long, dark tube. The walls around me smooth, covered in wet moss, no way to get out. When I woke up, sure as hell I'd pissed in the bed. My parents couldn't understand why. Nice people. Cause and effect? Not their strong point.

So I showed up at Forchtenstein around midday; the two cameras like bookends, with me in between. There was a little guardhouse just in front of the drawbridge over the moat. That's where I signed up for a tour of the fortress, with Herr Strobl listed as the guide. No trouble recognizing him when he showed up; red face, short and stocky. He had this snarly dog on a leash. A descendant of one of his war veterans? Strobl was decked out in a *Tracht*, one of those paramilitary uniforms Austrians love to parade around in. Come to think of it, not all that different from Uncle Emil's favorite outfit. Green, with epaulets and wood buttons, breeches leading down to long, red stockings. The whole ensemble topped off by a visored cap like you see on a chauffeur. A sign saying "Führer" stuck in the headband. (Easy there – that's just German for "guide.") A cheerful "*Grüss Gott*" to the eight of us on the tour. We trailed after him and the dog as they walked us through one room after another; chock-full of shields, lances, and standards, from the battles they fought there with the Turks in medieval times. He translated his patter into not-bad English when he found out I didn't understand German. How he *kvetched* about those cruel Turks! Looked all indignant when he talked about what they'd done to their prisoners. Many in the group looked stricken. Like what kind of barbarians could those invaders have been, not to stick to the Geneva Convention?

The well came last. When I saw it, don't think it didn't scare the shit out of me all over again. Didn't even dare to walk too near it. But when Strobl threw a burning piece of newspaper down the shaft, I edged closer. It took a long time for it to get to the bottom, the flickering light outlining the greenish-black walls. It must have been terrifying for the brides given the heave-ho.

When guides get that bashful look about them, you know it's the end of the session. Tipping time. Half expected the dog to get up on his hind legs, holding out a tin cup. The others in the group went up to shake hands with Strobl, one by one; dropping a coin into the palm they'd just squeezed. A couple of them even peeled off a bill or two. The bit about the bad Turks maltreating prisoners must have hit them in the wallet.

When it was my turn, I omitted the handshake and enlisted gravity to drop some change into his palm. No way I was going to touch this murderer. My laser was about to do the job for me. "Danke, danke" he beamed, as he and the dog were about to walk away. "Bitte, bitte," I smiled back, "may I take your picture?"

After giving Strobl's head my best shot, it was my turn to say "Danke." He was a cooked goose.

CHAPTER TWENTY
MORE PRIMATES

Early July, 1984

On the way back from Forchtenstein, I did a precautionary, no appointment necessary checkup on my psyche. Was I upset about what I was doing? If the answer was yes, I could always say to myself: "Sweetheart, are you OK? Anytime you want, you can pull out and go home. It's not worth getting yourself sick over it." Along the lines of the old adage, "A Jew belongs in a coffee house." But as far as I could see, I was doing fine. No regrets so far. You'd prefer a little more soul-searching from a man who makes other people bite the dust before they become dust themselves? Perhaps along the lines of maybe I should have given Strobl a reprieve, so he could live happily ever after with his dog? "Let healing (what a bullshit word, except if you're talking about a wound) take place"? No! I was just starting to enjoy myself. Thrilled about what these guys were going to be doing to themselves in a couple of weeks. Plus the kick of knowing something nobody else is in on, which makes serial murdering such an alluring hobby.

I planned to do Kleinert after lunch, and Baumgartner the next afternoon. There wouldn't be a lot of people hanging around the church at that time of day. I never did find out exactly what a lay brother does; what's his gig? Maybe they're like a *Gabbe* in a temple. The guy who hands out the prayer books, shaking his head as he shows you how far they're already along in the service. And here's late-sleeping you, dragging yourself in whenever it suits you.

Anyway, I got to this church on time. No sign sunk in the grass outside, identifying it as "So and So RC Church", Father Aloysius in charge, Father Antonio second-in-command. In a country like Austria, RC is taken for granted. The place looked Gothic and gloomy on the outside. Architecture as warning; if you don't believe in what's happening inside, it's your spiritual ass.

Not that I'm such a big expert on churches, but I like them on the empty side. Deserted, a church is the best no-price-of-admission theatre around. A few candles sputtering in the half-light. That smell of wax and incense, married to the special woody breath coming off all those old New Testaments wedged into the racks without an inch to spare. The insides of the spires so high, that they serve as a down payment for how unapproachable heaven really is. You never get rid of the feeling there's a stiff or two stuck in those damp stone walls, or maybe in those creepy-looking dark chests they have standing around. Where else can you walk right into a place where death, ascension, resurrection and force-feeding of body and blood substitutes take up the whole day, every day?

It took me a little while to get used to the dark. Asked myself, where do you start looking for a lay brother, especially between shows? Do they have a lounge, or a gym where they work out? Or do they attend classes, where they learn how to get rid of the "lay," with an eye to becoming truly paternal? A *Gabbe* you can always find. Either he's eating herring with sliced onion on rye bread in the lobby of the temple, or you'll find him teaching Hebrew to a bunch of Bar Mitzvah candidates, disguised as Cub Scouts.

The place was pretty much empty. Checked out the pews. A

couple of people kneeling, but not a sound out of them. Does anybody ever check the pulse, respiration and blood pressure of parishioners who stay in exactly the same position for, let's say, a week?

Nobody stopped me, so I just wandered around. I came upon a couple of guys in blue smocks swabbing down the stone floor, but neither of them looked like Kleinert. Then a priest walked by, dressed in summer whites; ditto. The boots were the tipoff when I finally caught sight of him. Shiny, black, and scary-looking as they protruded from under his brown cassock. For all I know, there's some special Vatican rule that excuses former Gendarmerie commanders from having to wear humble sandals. These gents might be needed to kick some serious ass any moment. He was crouching under a large Christ on the Cross, which hung from a small balcony overlooking the altar, while cleaning a silver Communion goblet with lots of elbow grease. Concentrating completely on the job, with a no-nonsense expression on his red face. Spit and polish. And I was about fifteen feet from him, trying to figure out what angle to use for my shot.

Asking Strobl to pose had made a lot of sense. But doing the same with Kleinert would have aroused suspicion. He still hadn't seen me, so I knelt down on the right side of the altar and pretended to focus the bogus camera on the huge hanging cross. Then I brought it down so as to get Brother Major Kleinert's behind-the-right-ear area in the perfect position. At which point, he scooted over to the other side, polishing everything in the vicinity like there was no tomorrow. Which there wasn't for him, if you look at the long view. So I had to pull the same reverent readjustment of the camera on the other side of the cross before I got my shot: the click and the answering hiss. Paydirt in about two weeks.

I took the rest of the day off. Went back to Vienna, took a long walk on the Graben and around the Hofburg. I hadn't fed anything to my Compulsive Bibliophilia Disorder since leaving New York. Now it pushed/dragged me into a couple of bookstores. In one, I bought some volumes in old German Gothic script, completely unreadable, but I liked the fancy bindings. In the other, before I knew it, I'd paid for the collected works of Stefan Zweig, in translation. As I was schlepping the heavy shopping bags back to Aunt Florence's house, I was in a good mood. My CBD was satisfied; at least for now. Besides, I was already looking forward to tomorrow, when I'd be zapping Baumgartner, my last candidate in St Marton.

The next day, no problem in finding his lumberyard on the outskirts of town. The street leading up to it was called Hans-Baumgartner-Gasse. Change the name after the war since the eponymous was a notorious Nazi? Not the St Marton way. The good old days might come back any time. No use being too hasty about taking down old street signs. Coming up to the lumberyard, I already heard lots of action and noise, which can be distracting for the amateur photographer. That annoying, whining sound coming from the kerosene-driven power saws was liable to break my concentration at a crucial moment. A guard stopped me at the gate. I kept saying "Baumgartner, Baumgartner" so often, that he waved me on, pointing to the door of an office. Baumgartner almost missed his destiny, at least for that afternoon. The office was empty. Just as I was leaving, a big white-haired guy with a red face comes running in, yelling. Sounded like what the fuck was I doing there? "Journalist, journalist," I cringed back, pointing to my cameras. Waved my New York State's driver's license in front of his nose, and recited something in German I'd memorized that morning. "I am writing for an American magazine, Confederate Carpenter, about old-time sawmills in the south of Austria. Everybody says this is THE place to take pictures." After my laborious spiel, Baumgartner showed a sudden, deep desire to shake my hand. A problem. That's when I got my arms tangled up in the camera straps. Direct contact consequently not possible. The rest was pretty easy. He showed me all around the place, and I took a great right-sided profile of the proud owner.

CHAPTER TWENTY-ONE
A HARD CASE

End of July, 1984

That left only Weissensteiner. The man who'd been in charge of the killing party at the jailhouse wall. I had his address in Wiener Neustadt, an industrial city around twenty or thirty miles from St Marton, where he was living with his daughter and her children.

I suspected all along he'd be a hard case. The others could all be found in some public place where I could get at them; even Hochberger who commuted between his old store and the tavern, two doors down, on a regular basis. From what I found out at the Chalfin Center, the one I was after now had no hobbies and spent most of his time cooped up at home. How was I going to get a shot at him?

He lived on a busy street. The first day, I had to spend a couple of hours looking at a newspaper I couldn't understand, in a little *Kaffeehaus* across the way, before I could get a good look at him. Even then, I only saw him for a minute, while he was taking out the garbage, dragging a cane.

Strobl, Kleinert, and the others had no real identity for me. They were just extras who'd helped Weissensteiner kill my father. For that, they were getting the punishment they deserved. But the last guy on the hit parade, number one on my wish list, was another story. Maybe I was reading into things, knowing what he had done – what he was capable of – but seeing him in person was even scarier than the visions I'd conjured up about him when I was a child. The tense way he carried himself, the jerky, abrupt movements. His head swiveling all the time, like a *Konzentrationslager* searchlight, to give his eyes the chance to make a full sweep.

The patients in the prison ward, at the County, charged with murder or aggravated assault, had that kind of look about them. But they were already in the can, with handcuffs for jewelry. Which meant whatever puss they put on, no way they could hurt you.

Keeping my distance from Weissensteiner, I went back to the same Kaffeehaus the next day, waiting for him to come out for another curtain call. Hoping this time he'd at least take a walk, or even go shopping, so I could follow him and somehow slip him the laser while he was in a crowd. Nothing doing. No wonder the guy was so pale. Just bringing the trash out once a day isn't guaranteed to give you a Florida tan. Had guilt made him a total recluse? Or shame? Any sign of remorse at all? Those tiny cups of muddy coffee that were keeping me company while I was doing my surveillance routine were beginning to give me heartburn. I started thinking up some weird scenarios, just to pass the time. For instance, how about me playing the Avon Lady? Knock, knock. "Hallo Herr Weissensteiner, can I interest you in something that will change your life forever?" Or I could set fire to his house in the middle of the night, and zap him while he's running out in his nightshirt, carrying his most precious possessions: a grandchild on one arm, and his old brown shirt with the swastika on the sleeve on the other.

The Avon Lady idea wasn't all that bizarre. I'd been right to do the anonymous bit – no real contact – with the others. The end result was all that mattered. Herr W., on the other hand, not in the same ballpark. What I needed was to make some kind of gesture, to give him that extra heads-up. To make him worry even more, especially once he started hearing about the suicides of some of his buddies. Every day, that much closer to getting carried out the door himself. (Same general idea as taking out the garbage.) I needed to give this one a hint of what was in store for him.

The time I spent casing the joint gave me a good idea of when I'd find him alone in the house. His daughter drove off with the kids at nine in the morning, came back around three. Nobody else ever went in or out. All I had to do was wait for her to leave, walk across the street, do my Avon Lady shtick, and be on my way.

When I was a kid, Weissensteiner would pop up in front of my eyes just as I was going to sleep. I was afraid he could come all the way to Ft. Lee, New Jersey, and do terrible things to my parents and me. Also to my dog Hugo. So, this guy and me had a past. The thought of meeting up with him spooked me the same as when he had the lead part in those waking nightmares of my childhood. Why was I so scared, I kept asking myself; what could he do to me? Lock me away in his attic, then march me down to his garden wall to be shot at dawn? This was an old guy! He couldn't even get around without a stick. But go try to convince your sweat glands and your intestines, just to name a couple of landing points for that special fear that floats around inside of you. The kind you don't even know where it's coming from. Go try to fight off a sneak attack like that. Remember Pearl Harbor.

What I needed right then was reinforcement – not theories – with some succor thrown in. A guy with a little Van Dyke beard, untidy white head of hair, and a worn black suit, ashes from his cigar giving it a fine, irregular, polka dot effect. That's who I could have used right then. With me stretched out over several café chairs transformed into a makeshift couch, and him saying, "Don't be such a *Hosenscheisser*. (trans.: a person with a cowardly anal sphincter.) Just go over there and let the motherfucker have it. Your father would *kvell* (trans.: a mix of pride and happiness) in his grave about having such a brave son."

Just a few minutes with the old gent would have made all the difference. But looking around, all I saw was the frock-coated waiter, reading the paper while picking his teeth (or vice-versa) and two eighty-year-olds playing chess. Staying in that Kaffeehaus, sweating profusely, was giving me cramps in my *kishkes*. What if my hero father had spun off a weenie? I could talk a good game, but deep down… when the going gets tough, just say you've had enough?

I went back to Aunt Florence's to take a long, hard look at my psyche, and what I was seeing wasn't pretty. But another walk around the city revived my will to kill. Brought on this time by taking a closer look at the plump, red-faced specimens filling the streets. Which invariably brings on the unanswerable question: Why us, and not them? Why are so many of us dead, while these clowns are still walking around, munching on crepes stuffed with whipped cream, the lather slobbering down their capacious chins?

The next day, after another few coffees, I asked Herr Ober, the overdressed waiter, for the bill. In Austria, the customer is expected to tote up his own order. (Just as I'd long been toting up what the Austrians owed me.) But I hadn't kept track of how many inky cups of coffee I'd had that morning. Now I had to translate the degree of heartburn into numbers, with Herr Ober standing over me, aggressively pushing air out through the gaps between his teeth.

After I was finally allowed to pay up, everything began to slow down. It felt like it took an hour for me just to cross the street. I don't remember reaching the other side, or even ringing the bell. But the next thing I knew, there was Weissensteiner standing in the doorway, looking straight at me. Same pissed off, wise-guy look, still some traces of the blond hair I'd seen in his picture. All I could do was blurt out his name, more an exclamation than a question. The quizzical expression on his face suggested he was wondering who the fuck I was, just like Baumgartner. They're really something, aren't they? No trouble finding six million Jews to kill, but can't spot a lone American executioner for beans.

A part of my brain must have got its wires wet from all those feelings sloshing around. Result: the lower centers, the ones around for millions of years, had to take over. The flight or fight question came up right away. The former must have won out, because, pathetically, I right away high-tailed it from the house to the corner. Weissensteiner must have sensed I wasn't just canvassing the neighborhood. For an old guy, he ran pretty fast, the old blood lust must still have been in him. Then he lunged at me, knocking me down. The safest thing seemed to be to just lie there for the moment, the twin cameras clutched to my chest.

Weissensteiner grunted in disgust, indifferent to the possibility that he'd cracked my skull. As he turned to head back to his house, I got my best photo opportunity of the week. Crazy angle, but by now I was a pro.

Nothing left to do except run after him, shouting the name "Brenner." Do bad boys like Weissensteiner keep track of their victims? Or were there too many to count?

Between St Marton and his time with the Wehrmacht in France, he must have had a hand in ending many people's lives: tortured them, deported them, executed them. What I needed to know was, did he remember his victims' names? Or at least my father's? With him, he might have lost his killing cherry. It's common knowledge everybody remembers their first. Of everything.

All I could do was to keep mouthing "Brenner" – by now in a low sob – over and over again. To feed him that name, like a slow-acting poison.

He didn't answer. Just stared at me, and I stared back. A pissing contest. Still not a word out of him. I gave up first, and turned away. As I was retreating down the street, I heard the door slam.

CHAPTER TWENTY-TWO
FURIOUS FLORENCE

End of July, 1984

It was getting to be Friday, and I was leaving Saturday. On Thursday, I could already see a change in Aunt Florence. You know how women let you know they're not happy? Big difference, in my experience, from showing you they're just plain unhappy; which may not even have anything to do with you in the first place. Not the same as the former, where it's usually something you're doing or not doing, take your pick. The corners of the mouth tighter, the touch cooler, the eyes less shiny. Right after that, you get withdrawal. No more holding on to you 24/7 like you're about to fall off a mountain any minute, excited about spending every possible moment with you. Your privileges are being cancelled, same as when your credit card maxes out. It's statistically likely you don't even know what brought about this change of weather in the first place.

Anyway, when I came out of my room Friday morning, I immediately understood I was in deep shit. Uncle Emil had already left, but Aunt Florence was still walking around in her *schmatte*. No peignoir to be seen. Breakfast as usual, except yesterday's dried-up bread, no poppy seed rolls. Therefore not the usual fallout. A subtle reminder there weren't going to be any graduation exercises under the piano. Aunt Florence distant. As if I was already far away; but, inconveniently, still around.

I figured it out pretty quick. I was leaving, that was the problem. As if I lived full-time in Vienna, and my only reason for taking off was to make her *platz* (trans.: bust.) Go explain you're just there on vacation. It seems pretty clear to me: if you're on vacation, you're not home; vice-versa also. But what's always in the air is an ugly little rumor: If you really wanted to, you could. But you don't, so you won't.

Austrian florist shops are all the same. Walk into them, right away you're in a jungle. Plants, gardenias, roses, etc. everywhere. The salespeople stuck behind a little tree in the back somewhere. Like Jap snipers in WWII. Why is the country so stuffed with flowers? What's with the glut? Thought about it for a while, and then it hit me. It must be because of the pileup of inventory during the war. A lot of citizens (guess who?) got sent far away from home, ended up dying there. According to the neighbors who stayed put, they wanted every which way to pay their respects. But – they keep claiming – there was no way of knowing if flowers were being accepted by the Konzentrationslager around then. How could they have followed their orders?

After a look around, I ended up choosing a big bouquet. Wrote sort of a dopey double entendre card to accompany it: "Thanks for having me. Your grateful nephew."

I carried the flowers back to the house. Sending them wouldn't have made the same impact. Show me an angry woman who doesn't soften up even a little bit when she's on the receiving end of a floral tribute. Aunt Florence was no different. Especially after reading the card. The corners of her lips loosened, and there was the merest glint in her eyes. Before the moment could fade, I went into my spiel. Meeting her all those years ago changed my life – also, her introducing me to Henry Miller – and made me understand, when I was a kid, what I could look forward to later on. Even more importantly, how many people get the chance to do it with the one they always dreamed of doing it with?

She didn't say much, while the glint in her eyes translated itself into a slow dribble of tears. Sure, she was sorry to see me go. But the waterworks must have come on because she remembered how young she'd been, at the top of her game, when she first met me such a long time ago. When I came to Vienna, she needed to update that memory. Offered me what she did best; like a souvenir.

No mention of the "L" word; then, as before. She understood I had to leave, that my brief furlough was up. But how could we keep alive the memory of what had gone on between us during those few hectic days? She didn't ask for much. She'd be content with long-distance pillow talk a couple of times a week. That was fine with me. I didn't want to break off abruptly with her either. At the last minute, I asked if we could continue the German lessons, translating the newspapers the way we'd already done. If everything went according to plan, Aunt Florence would be giving me the latest breaking news on the demise of the St Marton Five.

PART TWO

CHAPTER ONE

WAITING FOR PAYDIRT

Early August, 1984

Tell me one person in the whole world who wants to feel like a total asshole. What else would I be, if I go through this whole song and dance and come up with *bobkes* (trans: zero)? Surgeons are trained to act positive, even when the patient's family is about to make a coffee date with the funeral director. As things go from bad to worse, you can depend on us to be completely unrealistic about the patient's chances for survival. Same thing here. Brought up "if" – about the primates in Austria project – a couple of times in my own mind, but my bet was always on "when." Still, I kept having these notions about what would happen if the laser did the opposite of what I programmed it to do, gave my guys shock therapy instead. Stimulated the brains of the St Marton Five, but never got around to making them commit suicide. Kleinert graduating from lay brother to Archbishop in just a couple of months. After that, a shoo-in for Cardinal, with Pope right around the corner. Weissensteiner, so revved up by the laser, it made him into a bigger, even worse Hitler.

I always wondered who was going to be the first to break the ice. From my experience with the rats, I knew it didn't have to be strictly according to the zapping schedule. Sure enough, the next to the last became the first. Baumgartner, the sawmill guy.

Front page article in *Freies St Marton*. Aunt Florence read the whole thing to me over the phone a few days after I got back to New York. We translated it together. Gee whiz, we got ourselves a real sensational killing in this rube heaven. Reports from shocked eyewitnesses. The smell of something burning in Baumgartner's office. Found him with fire and smoke coming out of his mouth. A half-empty can of the kerosene they use for power saws, and a box of long fireplace matches next to him. By the time the ambulance showed up, he was already dead. Initial conclusion by Dr Heinrich, the first doctor on the scene: he took a big swig of the stuff and stuck a lit match into his mouth. The autopsy would tell us more. Aunt Florence moved on to the kind of obit a big citizen gets in a small pond. Husband, father, employer; all the good things he'd ever done. No mention of other activities considered very positive a long time before. How he helped run the Jews out of town, his role in the disappearance of Dr Brenner. Amnesia's not all bad. Especially if you keep just enough memory to remember what it is you want to forget. I was busting; that story gave me a big lift.

One of the five who killed my father got whacked for it. If my calculations were on the mark, the rest of the team was bound to follow. It was now just a question of when. Baumgartner doing what he did made me feel good in another direction too. There's a lot of talk about scientific curiosity, but it's a pretty curious scientist who doesn't feel great when he comes up with something nobody's ever latched onto before. In neurosurgery, when you work with the brain, you're always playing catch-up. Which means either you have to cut something out that's already there, or it's too late to do anything about it. But here, I got ahead of the game, made a brain do what I told it to do. To my relief, Baumgartner killed himself like the amateurs I'd met up with at the ME: aggressive, no namby-pamby. The other four would have to go to some lengths to beat him out for the award I'd be giving out at the end of the season. The Richard Brenner Prize for Creative Suicide.

Over the next few days, three more of my guys checked in. Actually, "checked out" is more appropriate. First Hochberger, found with his head, or what was left of it, in the grinder that produces hamburgers. The usual obit: blah, blah, blah. From what I could see so far, no tying up his suicide with Baumgartner's. Next to go was Kleinert. Hung himself on the big Christ on the Cross suspended over the altar in the St Marton church. He'd given me the photo-op when I zapped him. The rope looped around the cross, with his body hanging down, just about facing Jesus. A little bit of unease now creeping into the *Freies St Marton* account: like "Holy Shit! What's happening here?" I hadn't revealed to Aunt Florence anything about what I was really doing in St Marton. For all I knew, she was putting my visits there and the mysterious deaths in the same basket. Still, she didn't ask and I didn't tell. No use involving her.

After a couple of days, my man Strobl made his last appearance. Pretty big spread in the paper, especially since it happened at the fortress; also, the dramatic circumstances. First off, there was the dog moaning and barking next to the well, early in the morning. Somebody went to look for Strobl, but he'd disappeared. The dog kept jumping up onto the side of the well, so people took the hint and looked inside. Nothing suspicious to be seen, but, just to make sure, they sent a burning piece of newspaper down the shaft. It was stopped by Strobl's body, shoulders wedged into the wall, head submerged. Traditional kind of guy. Did to himself what they'd done to the brides of Forchtenstein. A real dive too—none of that feet first, squeezing your nostrils stuff.

Separate little article on page two. About the mysterious deaths of four well-respected citizens within days of each other. So far, all of them appeared to be suicides, but foul play was still a possibility. No clues yet, but watch this space. Pissed me off. Felt like sending an anonymous telegram to the St Marton police, set them straight. If you want clues, look next door to foul play. You dummies! Can't you see fair play when it's staring you in the face?

Leave it to Weissensteiner to hold out till the last minute, put a monkey wrench in my works. I was having *spilkes* (trans: ants in the pants, from anticipation) all the time about whether he'd managed to escape me at the last minute. I kept on rationalizing that four out of five wasn't so bad either. Which was, of course, horseshit. Herr W. was my main object all along. He was the star of my show, I couldn't do without him.

A while later, I got a first thing in the morning call from Aunt Florence. Not the usual time for our transatlantic German lessons/ pillow talk. First, the good news: Weissensteiner was found in the park, the one where the jail used to stand, with his throat cut, ear to ear. An old-fashioned razor clutched in his right hand. Now the bad news: he was still alive when a pedestrian accidentally stumbled on him. He was rushed to the hospital, where he was in "serious but stable condition." All this time, I hadn't considered the possibility that the assisted suicides might do what I programmed them to do, but that funny things could happen before the trip to the morgue. In other words, they might have the best of intentions to die, but still screwed up the process. What could I do now? Nothing, of course. I wasn't about to fly back to Austria and take another shot at his locus ceruleus. All I could do was hope that his attempted assassination of himself would give rise to complications. The kind we try to avoid in our postoperative patients, but which would be welcome in the case of Herr W. For a while, no news; either good or bad. But, just as he was ready to go home, he did the right thing. Jumped out the window.

The last of my father's executioners finally giving himself what he deserved. Final score: Max 5 – 0 St Marton murderers. Can't do better than that.

CHAPTER TWO

WHERE DO I GO
FROM HERE?

September, 1984

I don't have to tell you. Feel really good about something you've done, next thing you know, you're in negative territory. Thinking back to the glory days, but feeling like shit. That's the way I felt after the last of the St Marton Five (they should rest in pieces) bit the dust. The adrenaline that had been splashing around inside of me was just a puddle on the floor by now. I knew I had to do something with the laser, but what? Should I exchange neurosurgery for being a one-man Mossad, hunting down geriatric Nazis in remote corners of the world like La Gloria de Cucaracha, Paraguay? Or stick it to no-goodniks closer to home? Which could be a full-time job. I sat around a lot in my office, pondering these possibilities. I was back to work, but just about. Not paying much attention to the fledglings, who were starting to act like a dog who's been kicked once too many. My secretary, Marian, moping. The rats, chirping away to the tune of "kill me or experiment on me, but don't be indifferent."

In the end, I began to understand I wasn't cut out to be a freelance executioner. I'd had a score to settle with the St Marton murderers. Personal revenge is like having a suit made to order. Four buttons on the cuffs, a double vent in the back; refinements like that.

Not for everybody, but you get a big kick out of wearing it. Not the same as making yourself into a contract assassin, aiming for the locus ceruleus of people who deserve it, scattered throughout the world. Besides, doing bad to the bad carries its own risks. The bad are liable to take revenge. Which means you could stop living, for good; which is in itself bad. Or you can end up in jail. Which is not a good place to be stuck in.

No more killing, I vowed to myself. I owed it to the memory of my old girlfriend Eva, to keep the amateur suicides – like hers – to a minimum. Or, better yet, stopping them altogether. I knew how to burn down a suicide center. Now I had to think of a way to keep it from going into business on its own. Like those safecrackers who end up teaching everything they know to the Junior G-Men at the FBI Academy.

CHAPTER THREE
A SURPRISE VISIT

Late September, 1984

I never did get around to this new project of mine. It started off innocently enough. One afternoon, soon after I got back to New York, Marian told me Dr Kurastami was outside, wanted to see me right away. Also, there was a lady with him. When Marian says "lady," that's what you're going to get; not some bimbo camouflaged to look like one. What Persian Pete would be doing with such a specimen in tow was not in character. The women I'd seen him with, classy wasn't the first impression that grabbed you. More the opposite: smudged lipstick, gabbing away a mile a minute.

By then, he was already at my door, barging in as if he owned the place. Big 5 o'clock shadow, a lab coat over his scrub suit. Something funny about the outfit. A silk ascot around the neck, cascading down to cover the opening of the coat. Not part of the usual OR chic. Could be he hadn't had a chest haircut for a while, used the scarf to hide the evidence. And the lady? As soon as I saw her, my face turned as hot as if I'd stuck my head inside an oven; together with a pulsating headache, suggesting my blood pressure must have soared in an instant. It was Alison Hamilton. I hadn't seen her since the day she showed me around the Chalfin Center. Within seconds, that urgent need to talk to her *ad infinitum*, to eat her whole and especially certain of her component parts, and to impregnate my nose with her smell came back to me. The Penile Paradox, my usual Johnny-on-the spot, not far behind. When I was with Aunt Florence, also when I got back to my current social worker, Elena I, at the point of the *petite mort* – leave it to the French to downgrade an orgasm not into the death we all fear, but its junior partner – all I could see was Alison in front of me. Together with a momentary osmic hallucination. My nose fooled into catching the whiff she gave off – toes wrapped in lotion meeting expensive leather – that day in the stairway leading down from Lynx's office. Talk about paradoxes. I didn't have a hope of getting it up with her, but just the thought of her while I was with other people gave me a big jolt in the Marlboro Man direction. I'm all for delving into the roots of words. Finding out where they come from, how they've evolved over the centuries. In the case of Alison, maybe that's why they call it "prick."

She'd been on my mind ever since the moment Lynx introduced us. Before going to Austria, I'd tried to get in touch with her. I kept phoning, left messages, but never got a call back. That didn't stop me. Even tried to storm the Chalfin Center, but couldn't get in the door. No appointment, no admission. All I was left with were scenarios cooked up by my mind. Bumping into her on the street, when she feels a sudden *coup de foudre*. The electric shock you feel when THE ONE comes along, when you've stuck your finger in just the right socket. Or another improbable event: she's been thinking about me ever since Lynx introduced us. Tried to control herself, stay cool. In the end, she couldn't help herself. Called, and confessed she'd been crazy about me all along. Most nights, I'd be rocking myself to sleep, picturing these impossible possibilities.

But what I never expected was for her to show up in my office, accompanied by Persian Pete. What was she was doing here with that jerk?

She wore a peasant-type blouse, which must have cost what ten peasants get for a year's work. Complemented by a light beige skirt dropping to a couple of inches above the knees, made of the kind of linen that's crumpled on purpose. Great outfit all around. Hair still piled high on her head, which was slightly inclined forward, nodding halfway. As I was helping her into the only available chair (Persian Pete got to sit on the packing case with the rat food), I detected a solitary drop heading down to her right popliteal fossa. That's the delicious carved-out parking space behind the knee; a great spot to give your tongue a rest after it's through gliding up and down a woman's leg. Made me wonder where the drop started out from. A Darwin moment.

I'll never forget the first thing she said to me that day. When she opened her mouth, it was curtains for me. There's always a split-second when your life takes a sharp turn. No particular reason to think so at the time, but it turned out that way. One thing led to another, which is how I ended up here.

"I'm told," she says to me with an impersonal little smile – the kind you give the doorman when you ask him to walk your dog – while putting her hand lightly on P. Pete's arm, "that suicide is your special field of interest."

I'd just witnessed the kind of up-close-and-personal dermatology that's so hard to take, when it's between a woman you want to eat up alive, and a guy you want to offer to the nearest available alligator. It also brought up some urgent questions. How did she meet Pete in the first place, and was there anything up between them? Had she already heard about the St Marton Five, was that why she was sitting in my office now? And if the answer to the last question was yes, did she suspect I had something to do with it? Or was she just on a fishing expedition, with Pete playing the worm at the end of the hook?

"Yes," I admitted.

"What about the rats," she wanted to know, making small talk. "Do they figure in on the research?"

"Yeah, but on a very basic level," I lied. "To compare their anatomy with human anatomy." Then I told her what Pete already knew from my reports to the Department. That there's a burnt-out area in the brains of certain suicides. "I'm trying to put it all together, but who knows if it's ever going to lead to anything." End of story. Standard modest scientist bulletin from the front lines. Doing my best, but can't promise results.

Now it was my turn. Just as Baumgartner asked when I invited myself into his office: what the fuck are you doing here? Didn't put it exactly like that, but Alison and Pete caught my meaning. They'd met at a party a couple of weeks before, and she mentioned the puzzling series of suicides in Austria. Her contacts over there knew that all the departed had season tickets in her filing system, so they filled her in on the news. What she couldn't understand was why they did themselves in so many years later. Something else she found fishy: why all around the same time? Akbar had told her about me and my research. For sure, I'd be able to help.

She didn't put two and two together until she actually saw me. That we'd already met; no introduction necessary. That time at the Chalfin Center, she didn't even ask what I did for a living. To which, I thought, because you couldn't care less, playing the Shabbes Goy Prom Queen. Now she was about to bat her baby blues in my direction, hoping for some answers.

I couldn't blame her for trying to get information wherever she could. But Pete was another story, showing me off like the organ grinder's monkey. While, knowing him, all he cared about was grinding his organ. The creep. Figured it was time to send out a false lead. I had to get her off my case quick, before she put two hundred rats and five dead Nazis together.

Went into the mass hysteria routine. What you read in the papers now and then, about teenagers in the same high school killing themselves. Happy, cheerleaders, jocks. Nobody ever finds out why. Also, told her about an article in a Russian psychiatry journal, about some old army buddies doing the same thing. Ditto, why they did it. What I told her about the Russians was a complete fabrication. Hoped she'd take my word for it, not ask for the reference. I then threw in a bit about collective guilt. "Who's to know these Austrians you're talking about didn't get together for an evening of drinking? Talking about the past gave them all such an attack of low self-esteem, they couldn't live with themselves anymore."

She didn't say a word while I was going through my act, but began to look more and more serious. She was going to have to figure this one out by herself. Meanwhile, Pete was turning glum. With the puss of a guy who brings his three-year-old to a could-have-a-prodigy-on-my-hands piano competition, and all the kid can do is make in his pants. I'm still not sure what he expected. Get the mystery solved in a jiffy? Drop everything so I could help her out?

As they were leaving, I couldn't help but notice the little pat she planted on his ass. Looked to me like it wasn't the first time.

CHAPTER FOUR

SPANISH FLIES

October, 1984

That night, before going to sleep, I had a waking dream. That happens to me sometimes. A newsreel playing in my mind.

After the first bottle of wine at dinner, they were already very palsy-walsy. He bet her a dollar she wouldn't go to the ladies' room, take off her panties, and bring them back to him so he could sport them in his handkerchief pocket. Which she did, in a doggie bag graciously provided by the management. The fancy Scandinavian restaurant was on the ground floor of the house where he lived, so they didn't have far to go to take the elevator up to his apartment. Self-service, nobody else around. As soon as the door slid shut, he had her halfway down on the ancient, red plush seat, licking her neck and ears with his Aquavit-soaked tongue. Then dropping down to her nipples, which were starting to draw more and more attention to themselves through her thin blouse. He was just about to push the emergency stop button, when they reached his floor. Private landing.

Quickly into the living room where – it was a cool evening – a fire was burning. In front of the massive marble chimney, there was a big multicolored rug, with any number of what looked like little antennas coming out of it. Pete didn't miss a beat, and continued where he'd left off. Again started working his way down to the nipples. By then, the buttons had already popped off her blouse, which was jettisoned in a hurry. No bra to delay the proceedings. Getting rid of her wrap-around skirt was next on the agenda. There are two known ways to remove these. Either the one helping with the undressing walks around and around – like those camels in North Africa – or the wearer goes into a whirling dervish act. Ended up a little of both. Pete walked a couple of circles, and she twirled some. Result: the skirt ended up on the floor like a shroud, with the result that Alison was lying naked on the carpet.

Not just any ordinary carpet. This rug was 100% made up of Spanish flies. Which are very hard to come by, since they mostly go up in a puff of smoke right after they release their liquid. That's the Spanish Fly you kept on hearing about as a kid. The potion that's supposed to throw you into sexual overdrive as soon as you drink it. An inferior product, nothing like the flies themselves.

There she was, spread out on the rug. Those little stand-up things that looked like antennas (actually, the flies' legs) tickled her every which way. They played a little overture for her, while the conductor was getting ready to take his opening bows.

They can deny it all they want, but it's a fact. People check each other out the first time they go to bed. They may act like they're blinded by passion, but still, they don't miss a trick. Didn't expect her to have gray pubic hair; are his testicles undescended, or what? Buyer's remorse. But what Alison saw when Pete took off his pants made her speechless. Can't blame her. He had the kind of equipment that could easily qualify for a National Endowment Award. Not only that, but it took just a few seconds for it to stretch to a full 180 degrees. Made me wonder if he wasn't drinking the solution he made out of the post cingulate cortexes of his mice.

Giving him this world-class hard-on.

When he got on the carpet with her, the legs began agitating in every which direction, while making a whirring sound. They were playing games with her now. Threading their way into tiny – and not so tiny – spaces. Beating away – sometimes alone, sometimes together – at spots on her rear end. Mini-spankings.

I'd been naïve, when I first saw them together, to wonder what was up between them. Now, it hit me right between the eyes. His centipede-without-legs sauntering and slithering its way right through her vestibule onto the living quarters. Its trajectory helped along by jets discharging all around, like an automatic car wash. Spraying out the salty tears of joy wept by the sisters Bartholin, who were watching the proceedings like the twin lions at the entrance to the New York Public Library.

If you didn't know better, the centipede was acting like it wasn't sure how far it wanted to go. Kept moving in, then coming halfway out again. Alison started yelling "yes" every time it happened. Pete playing cat and mouse with his centipede, Alison now wailing "more" between each "yes." Listened hard for the question, but all I heard was what sounded like an answer. Made me think of Onkel Sigi Freud, who addressed himself to one of the fundamental questions of all time: What do women want? Not that he ever came up with a good answer to his own question. In that brief moment, I tried to hook up the answerless question with the questionless answer that kept bouncing up and down in front of me.

By now, the situation was rapidly going downhill. Meanwhile, Pete not saying anything. As much of a loudmouth as he usually is, he's quiet and deliberate in the OR. That's the way he was now. Didn't seem to bother her any. By this time, she was screaming so loud, she couldn't have heard him anyway. All along, the Spanish legs going at it nonstop. Making her do a Fandango, or maybe a Tarantella on that carpet. Gotta hand it to her. You try to dance, pinned down like she was.

Pretty soon, I heard this muffled little explosion. Like when they detonate a bomb under water. She was having a convulsion. I've seen a lot of them in my work. Arched her back, threw her head around. Still dancing on her back. Yelling blue murder, words I couldn't understand.

Afterwards, dead quiet. Even the Spanish legs calmed down. Alison and Pete gulping and breathing fast, like when you've been under water for too long. Then a popping sound, the one that comes from two sweating skins pulling apart, breaking the vacuum.

So, what do you talk about with a stranger during the time that turns out to be either between or after? With or your wife or girlfriend, an opportunity to discuss important things. Has the gardener been by yet?; or, what are we doing next weekend? Close-to-the-heart stuff like that. But with somebody you've just introduced yourself into, it's not as if you can get up and applaud, or quickly run down and buy a bunch of flowers. Making small talk after something big has happened is tough. What's left then? A lot of stretching, with a dumb grin on your face. Every few minutes, huddling and cuddling.

Not only that, but plenty of "wow," "amazing," and "you're the best." Meanwhile, keeping an eye out for the suspense to end. Either goodbye for now, or happy days are here again.

The latter was what happened here. Couldn't tell who started it off this time. Now it was all Alison's show. My mind doesn't own a telephoto lens, so I don't know how much Pete was contributing. Still, quick like a bunny, she went operative. Got on all fours, and right away bent her head down.

That hit me where I live. How could I have been so slow all along? To miss what was wrong with her neck? That steady nod was there from the very beginning. Should have picked up on it, even then. What one of our neurologists, Al Quicksilver, baptized "cocksuckers' neck." Called it something less graphic, "Fellatio-Related Neck Derangement" in the article he wrote about it.

Mystery solved. From what I could see, her act pretty routine, except the end was a little special. Alison was just about to capture the rapture, when her lungs called for a split-second time out. Which made Pete waste his seed all over a corner of the carpet. Like when your home run is called back because the guy on first base needs to tie his shoelaces. Right away makes the Spanish legs do a wave, like they're fans at the ballpark. Now, all of a sudden, Alison and Pete have a lot to talk about. "I'm so sorry," "it's OK," "it's not OK," "really, it is OK." Next, she's offering him a rain check. He couldn't help but accept, the greedy bastard. But always the gentleman. The Aer Lingus flight started taxiing down the runway, about to take off any minute. Anybody's guess, how long this Alphonse and Gaston routine was going to take. J.S. Bach was right on the money with his cantata "Ich habe genug." My feelings exactly. Time to turn off the projector.

CHAPTER FIVE

LET'S HEAR IT FROM THE KOLOSVARER REBBE

October, 1984

Pete and me, we have a history. Remember how he took away Rosie, the red-headed secretary with the major epilogue and prologue? But fucking around with my fantasy woman, that's where I draw the line. The Alison in my head was off-limits to everybody. Just because I couldn't have her, didn't mean she wasn't mine. From what I could see, Pete was guilty of breaking and entering. Or did she unlock the door, and Pete didn't need to break it down? Think of it this way. First he stuffs her with exotic foreign drinks, then he forces her to drop her panties. In public! Also, he hypnotizes her into taking off her dress by walking around her, slower and slower. Ended up throwing her down on the carpet and forcing himself on her. What choice did she have? She had to submit. Who knows what he might have done if she'd resisted?

OK, that permanent nod, her head bent forward all the time, that doesn't make her sound like much of a greenhorn in the sex department? Still, that all happened before I met her. Now she's mine. Even if no way am I hers.

I've been bending your ears about my fantasy woman. Still, that doesn't mean that what happened between Alison and Pete was a fantasy too. But since the whole scene played out only in my mind, how do I know for sure they did what I saw them do? Here's a last-minute tip from the sainted Kolosvarer Rebbe. "How do you know they didn't do it?" he mused, when he pronounced judgment at the end of some long-forgotten dispute brought to his court.

Go top that.

CHAPTER SIX

REVENGE FANTASIES REDUX

Early November, 1984

I already told you about the decision I made when I came back after the St Marton caper: to lay off social engineering for good. No more killing baddies. Making their suicide center dance to my tune. Turning off the electricity this time around. Giving people a chance to live, instead of knocking themselves off because the suicide center was having a bad day.

But what I'd just witnessed put an end to my good intentions. Seeing Pete in action with Alison put a new itch in my trigger finger. Even if I shot the laser at him, that wouldn't get Alison scurrying over to my corner. I understood that. But what I was really after was revenge. The same as what I felt about the St Marton murderers, even though Pete's crime was just a minor misdemeanor compared to theirs. By now, his very existence hurt my feelings. Seeing him, or even just knowing he was somewhere around, would always remind me the difference between us. For me, he was a jerk. Still, there was no escaping the truth that women flocked to him. That exotic accent, the carpet with the tickling flies, and the size of his member—mine wouldn't have minded being part of that exclusive club—made him irresistible. I had a monopoly on my social workers, but that was small change in comparison. Alison was a big fish, and he'd hooked her in no time.

The rush I'd felt in St Marton, when I was all ready to do in the local Murder Inc., was coming back to me now. I could see it all in front of me. Offering to take a nice sideways snapshot of the soon-to-be-late Persian Pete. Then waiting a couple of weeks for him to take a jump from his office window, or put a plastic bag over his head. Any way he wanted; I'd leave him the choice. Afterwards, offering Alison a shoulder to cry on, big-brother style. The Chief declaiming some bullshit about how Pete was a fallen soldier on the battlefield of science. Revenge rearing its beautiful head. Getting back at him for Alison. Also for Rosie, the secretary with the unforgettable ass; another putdown for me. Not to speak of making a laughing stock of the very project that was now about to kill him.

In Hollywood, they do sequels of old-time blockbusters. This was my sequel to the St Marton scenario. The fake camera was doing cartwheels on top of the filing cabinet. Raring to go.

CHAPTER SEVEN
ALISON CONFIDENTIAL

Mid-November, 1984

Shooting the laser at people takes planning. If you want to kill somebody, aiming the gun in the general direction of the head or the chest, that's enough to do the job. But with my weapon, just behind the right ear is the place you have to hit. I'd proven that with the rats and the primates with the Tyrolean hats, so that's what I had to do with Pete. Which meant I had to figure out the right place and time to administer the shot. With no witnesses around, goes without saying.

One morning, while I was doping out the logistics, Alison sashays into my office. No Pete this time around. She was in the neighborhood, just wanted to say hello. Yeah, tell it to the Marines. She had on this bland puss that women wear when they're about to fuck you over. When it's the same words but without the "over," facial maneuvers all different. Dreamy look, drooping lids; giving you a preview of the immediate future.

Her hair was down, no upsweep this time around. Shiny, above-the-knee silk dress clinging to her, discreet flowers in a pattern designed to identify her major landmarks. The whole package putting out a perfume which momentarily improved the atmospheric conditions of my smelly office.

As she was sitting across from me, legs straight out, there was another fragrance that called attention to itself. The Underskirt Factor. It's not a big topic of conversation, but it can be a real deal maker – or breaker – in sex. Because it's not only what reaches your nose that counts, but what your brain makes of it. So, if a woman really turns you on, just the slightest hint coming from that general direction echoes in your brain. Meanwhile, the other noses in the vicinity don't notice a thing. Like when they use dogs to pick up on the scent of guys who just busted out of jail.

I read an article a while ago about a study in which they did some fancy mathematics and came up with a number which could not only tell you *if* you loved somebody, but also *how much*. All the way from an Underskirt Factor of 1, which means just about, to a 5, which is in the crazy-about range.

I'd only seen her twice before. I knew very little about her. Just what she did for a living and her academic credentials. Maybe that was better than getting involved in the nitty-gritty of her everyday life. Let's say, she's a virago around the time of her periods, or a gastronomic menace in the kitchen. So far, I'd spent a lot more time fantasizing about her than actually being face-to-face with her. Still, no need to tell you what her Underskirt Factor rating was for me. Too bad more men don't know how the right whiff can tip you off about who's the one for you. Also, how it can save you a lot of grief, if you catch on to the vice-versa.

She got to the point in a hurry. Batting her baby blues, coming to see me accidentally on purpose. Doing her all-business hoochy-koochy, with me as an audience of one. Made me realize she'd caught on to how I felt about her from the very beginning. So now I was going to have to pay the price, by giving her information.

Exactly what kind, was bound to come out any minute.

Did I remember, the last time she was here, when we talked about suicide? In relation to the five Austrians who'd done themselves in, to be exact? Yes, I did remember. Mind you, not that she was sorry they were dead. Why they did it; that's what still puzzled her. In the meantime, she'd gotten more info from her Austrian contacts. Who, she didn't say. I riffed on that for a few seconds. A Manchurian Candidate in the St Marton police? A plant belonging to the Chalfin Documentation Center, waiting for just this opportunity to justify the long-term investment?

For a few days in the summer, a foreign type was seen in the center of St Marton. Nondescript looking, thick glasses; very average. Wearing hushpuppies and a baseball cap. Smiled a lot, the way Americans do when they can't speak the local language. Carrying two big cameras, one on each shoulder. He'd been spotted outside Baumgartner's sawmill, also in front of the local church. Someone even remembered him from a tour group led by Herr Strobl up in the fortress, in Forchtenstein. The accurate reportage sounded like the Mossad to me. Israelis, posing as local yokels, the accent down pat. Trolling for info, as if they were fishing in the Red Sea. Sending the whole package special delivery – like lobsters wrapped in ice – to the mastermind Super Shikse in New York.

One way to wriggle out of this was to play dumb. "Why are you telling me all this?" I asked. "I may have a professional interest in suicide, but no way am I a detective." "Listen," she says, "Akbar has been telling me about what you call 'amateur suicides.' The ones who do it from one minute to the next. That's exactly what happened with these Austrians."

She was onto something. A guy who could well be me, hanging around a little town. Pretty soon, five local citizens bite the dust by their own hand. You don't have to be Inspector Maigret to figure that one out. She had me dead to rights, but she still had no clue about how I did it. I was playing for time, so I came up with a question of my own. I was ready to admit to her that I was somehow responsible for those bizarre deaths in St Marton, but it would have to be in exchange for what I urgently needed to know.

"You'll find out soon enough what happened over there," I answered, "but I have a question of my own. Exactly what's up between you and Akbar?" She looked taken aback. Here she was busting her ass to solve a mystery, and I was being a busybody, digging for inside dope on her love life. Still, she must have understood that this was going to be a quid pro quo. Answer my question, and she'd get some answers of her own.

"We're close," she says in a little girl voice. "I'm crazy about him."

What Alison saw in this greaseball, I'll never know. The only possibility I could think of was what I saw that night in the newsreel in front of me, when he dropped his pants.

Her answer made me feel like a total schmuck. Here I'd been telling myself stories about how Pete had ravished her that time with the Spanish flies, but it turned out she'd been a willing accomplice all along. No way was I ever going to capture her for myself. I'd have to settle for her being – and staying – at the top of my fantasy wishlist.

"Why do you want to know?" she added, almost as an afterthought.

I had nothing left to lose; no reason to play coy. "Because as crazy as you are about him, that's how crazy I am about you."

What could she say? Not much. Just how flattered she was about my feelings. How she could see being friends with me in the future. That was the gist of her sending me a noncommittal "thanks, but no thanks."

Now that I'd gotten my answer, I went back to the reason she was here in the first place.

"You're on the button," I admitted, "the guy with the hushpuppies was me."

"But how did you do it? How did you get rid of these guys?" she wanted to know.

My head felt like it was about to pop open.. The morning had already been a disaster. Her confession, my confession; my blown cover in St Marton, when I thought I was being so clever. I told her I needed some time to think, that she'd get some answers pretty quick. She must have understood she wouldn't get any more out of me right then. Said she'd drop by again in a few days. I promised to come up with the goods she was looking for.

As she was going out the door, she casually sent a few words in my general direction. "Hope nothing happens to Akbar. It's not his fault I love him so much!"

CHAPTER EIGHT
PETE GETS A REPRIEVE

November, 1984

While I was waiting for Alison to come back, I had another big worry. I'd just gotten the final judgment from the Housing Court. My books and me were found guilty on all counts. No wonder: the owner (that illiterate jerk) had brought along a couple of experts who swore that the weight of my book-stuffed apartment was tipping the building to one side. That must have convinced the judge. We had to leave by the end of the month. I didn't care about myself, I could always sleep in my office; at least for the time being. But what about the books being torn out of the only home they'd ever known? I might have to rent a storage unit and visit them on Sundays, like a single dad. I just couldn't face it.

My new social worker, Elena I, tried her best to console me. Her shtick was to put on an old-time nun's habit (she'd purloined it during a brief stint in an upstate convent) before the main event. Then we'd go into our number with the outfit on or off every which way. For minutes on end, it was night in the daytime, while I was wrapped up in the folds of that black tent. Gotta admit, those religious exercises gave me what's called "symptomatic relief."

The last words Alison said hit me right in the *kishkes*. Her coming to the conclusion that the five suicides were somehow engineered by me didn't bother me. If anything, I welcomed the chance to show off to her. To prove that the forgettable guy in the hushpuppies had another, enigmatic, unsuspected side to him. But she'd gone further, used those Princeton smarts. If I somehow got rid of the St Marton bad boys, what was to prevent me from doing the same to Pete? Nothing. That's why she sent me that veiled little warning. Which meant: I'm on to you, keep your murderous mitts off my Akbar.

Now I had a real dilemma on my hands. I was going to punish Pete because he'd forced himself on her, made her do all that steamy stuff I'd seen in my mind's personal newsreel. Now it turned out she was a collaborator with the regime, not a victim as I'd thought. When she got up on all fours and stuffed her mouth with as much as she could get hold of, he wasn't holding a gun to her head. Far from it. I'd have gone through with my plan to zap him with the laser because he'd forced my #1 Shikse Fantasy Princess into what used to be called "unnatural acts." Turned out they were anything but unnatural for either of them. I was ready to do my social engineering stunt one last time to punish Pete for what ended up to be just a misunderstanding. Sure I was jealous of him, also what the two of them were up to. But he hadn't forced her into anything. To kill him now would just make me a murderer, same as the ones who killed my father.

Which left a big hole in my schedule. I could always go back to cutting the suicide center down to size by keeping the amateurs from going all the way. Research can be a refuge: ponder away for all your're worth, meanwhile not getting your hands dirty. But now that I was dropping the doing-away-with-Pete project, I needed something to take its place. You can't just hope that the energy you've generated in your mind – and decided not to use at the last minute – will take the hint and float away somewhere, take you off the hook. It'll keep knocking on your door, until you slot it into something else you're doing; or at least thinking about.

Which is exactly what happened with me. For a while, I'd been considering being my own guinea pig. Not stop with just the theory of how the suicide center works, but go all the way, try it out on myself.

In medicine, self-experimentation happens more often than you'd think. What you discovered could be dangerous, so you don't want anybody else to take the risk. Also, how many cooks do you know, who don't want – need – a healthy taste of what they concoct? Still, the lead-up to killing myself, not death itself, was the main attraction. What really goes on, just before? Do you become hypnotized by the burnt-out suicide center? Feet, hands, or whatever is going to work best, in a trance? Can't resist opening the window, fiddling with the rope, no will of your own?

No way of knowing for sure how the whole thing works, until it actually happens to you. By then, it might be too late to send a picture postcard. But just think of that moment of revelation, when everything's falling into place. How many people do you know of, who can die on their own specific terms? Not just killing themselves; anybody can do that. But having their suicide center tickled into doing the job? That's an original.

Sound a little over the top, to think all at once of ending it all? (Or beginning it all, you never know…) It sure sounds suspicious, making a decision like that in what sounds like one moment to another. But think of it this way: it only *seems* like you made up your mind in an instant. Actually, the thought behind it has been laying low, taking its own sweet time. Then along comes a catalyst – a spark – and you get what appears to be a snap decision.

Same with me. Trying out the invention on myself was always percolating away in the background. Could be I was never going all the way with it, but the whole Alison business put it over the top. I was ready to die *for* love, which is not the same as dying *from* it. You're racing to a motel for a rendezvous – you can't wait another minute to do what you're going there for in the first place – and you get killed in a car crash on the way. Love is what pulled you in; not its fault you can't drive straight. In that situation, the feeling, the desire is mutual. Not the one-sided mooning around engaged in by yours truly towards Alison. Dying *for* love fits much better into that equation. Letting it – helping it – clobber you over the head.

But pointing the laser at my own head, pulling the trigger? Not that anybody was checking, but I still had a protocol to follow. Just because you're planning to get yourself killed, doesn't mean you can dump the science you've been fed all your adult life. No; somebody had to do it to me, let my suicide center take over from there.

Who else but Alison?

CHAPTER NINE

A TASTE OF MY OWN
MEDICINE

Late November, 1984

She showed up right on schedule a couple of days later. A purposeful look about her. No more playing coy. Now was the time to cough up the info I'd promised her. I'd moved the two cameras down from the shelf onto my desk. No way she could miss them. As soon as she walked in, I could see her focusing on them. The cameras had to be a tipoff for her. "Aha," she must have been thinking, "now I've got him by the short hairs." After that, no more asking for help; on the order of, we're fellow dicks trying to crack this case. Now it was me getting the third degree. She knew already that I'd lugged around two cameras when I was spotted in St Marton. What make were the cameras, why did I need two? She'd find out soon enough, but, for the moment, I acted puzzled. Like what a crazy idea, to incriminate those innocent cameras.

I offered to open them up, show her what's inside. That put a little red on her face. She was getting ready to apologize, when I took the real camera out of its case. Clicked the shutter, shot off the flash. Then I showed her the exposed film inside, so she could see it was all on the up and up. By this time, she was already embarrassed. Wanted me to stop, she believed me, no use going on with this. But I insisted, protesting I had nothing to hide. That's when I handed her the fake camera, the one carrying its secret pregnancy, the laser.

By now you could ask, didn't I have some last minute doubts about what I was doing? If I was going to have her feed me a poison, there'd always be an antidote, in case I changed my mind. But once she shot the laser at me, there was no going back. As far as I knew, no way you can cut a deal with a suicide center. Dicker back and forth, negotiate something. Once you're in, no way of getting out. I was getting myself killed because this particular woman couldn't care less whether I lived or died. On top of my being so nosy that I had to follow my research until the very end. That's why I couldn't back out now.

So there I was, showing her the second camera, the fake one. I already had her on the defensive, so I kept pushing her, how she had it all wrong with the cameras. Offered to let her take a snapshot of me. Supposing this was some kind of death ray Brownie, would I be crazy enough to let it shine on me? She kept saying no, no, no. (If only she'd just once said yes, yes, yes to me, I wouldn't be in the predicament I'm in now.) I kept insisting. Showed her the shutter button, and how to focus on my right-sided profile. The one with the active locus ceruleus.

When she finally clicked the button, no flash; also, no sound from the shutter. Just a short, low hiss, and a tiny little burning smell. She understood right away what had happened, what I'd made her do. Came right over and put her arms around me, the waterworks instantly turned on, saying "you poor boy, you poor boy," over and over again. Planted her mouth on my cheek, and left a little puddle of spit mixed with tears, to mark the spot. Made me resolve never to wash that side of my face again. No question it was an extreme way to get her attention. Is it a fair tradeoff to die in exchange for a wet kiss?

CHAPTER TEN

THE TRUTH MAKES ME FREE (SORT OF)

Early December, 1984

So, if the suicide center is supposed to do the job within a few days of getting zapped, what am I still doing here? Shouldn't I be way dead by now? The answer to the latter question is "yes." Which brings up an urgent consideration: how am I different from the five I've already put away? We all got the laser beam shot in the general direction of our right locus ceruleus, and I'm the only one who's still around to tell the story. Is it professional courtesy extended by my suicide center? Could it be it can't stand to put away the guy who first put it on the map?

What went wrong was, I got stopped from going through with what's supposed to happen next, after the center gets burned. The arms and legs executing the execution after the usual incubation period. You can't hang it on the laser not working, or Alison not aiming at the right spot. I was the only one to blame for what happened afterwards. I spilled my guts to Alison. I've asked myself why a hundred times, and I still don't know the answer. People do crazy things after going through a big emotional calamity. How much more emotional can it get, than when you trick the woman you dream of – even when you're awake – jolting your suicide center into action? Or maybe there's even a simpler explanation. The brain is a dark attic stuffed with info you want to keep to yourself. Maybe it just felt good to open the little window, let in some light and air.

What I should have 100% for sure have shut my trap about, was the usual timing between the locus zap and the actual suicide. If I hadn't let Alison in on that, I wouldn't—at least for the time being—be sentenced *to* life. Nothing to do with being sentenced *for* life. The ones involved in the latter activity hope to walk out the front door of the prison someday. In my case, parole means I'll be going through with what my suicide center was programmed to do all along.

Meanwhile, Alison was going on and on about how guilty she was feeling. After all, she was the one who pulled the trigger. Kept reassuring her it wasn't her fault. I'd conned her into doing it.

She asked me to sit tight, she'd be back within the hour. Did I promise I wouldn't leave, do anything silly? Which is a laugh. I mean, how much more could I have upped the ante, after what I made happen a little while before? I had no idea what she was up to, but there was one thing I had to do right away: get rid of the laser gun, the paperwork, and all the research notes about how the suicide center operates. If I died, or something went wrong and I stayed alive, no way I was going to let anybody else in on what I'd figured out. Who knows what would happen, if anybody got hold of my invention? Use it for stickups. "Hands up, or your locus is dead meat!" And, how about in politics? Knock off our government, and replace it with a traveling squad of North Koreans? It was my patriotic duty to Our American Way of Life not to let the technology fall "into the wrong hands."

Didn't take long to break the laser and the fake camera into little pieces. I dumped the wreckage into the garbage can down the hall, then burned my notes in the lab sink. Lively little bonfire. The rats enjoyed it; jumped up and down, like it was the village fair.

INSIDE THE COUNTY PSYCHO

Early December, 1984

Nowadays, the Psycho Unit at the County is all different from what it used to be. In the old days, there were any number of crazy people in there. They got sent in from all over the city, making it a way station for acting weird. Threatened to kill their family, or even went through with it; citizens walking the streets in their birthday suits. That kind of bad behavior. Then they'd get funneled out again, either for another chance back home, or to the State Hospitals, which were holding pens for the ones who were never going to get better. These days though, having something go wrong with your head doesn't get you three squares and a clean bed. Instead, you get a shithouse full of pills, and, if you have no other place to go, you get to sleep on the street. Making the County, and other public hospitals, pioneers in the out-of-doors treatment of schizophrenia.

Doesn't mean they closed the Psycho – that's what everybody's always called it – down altogether. They kept a VIP floor for people they want to "keep under observation." Which means if you're important enough and you've gone off the rails enough, that's your temporary refuge. Me, they've got in the penthouse suite. Nice view of the smokestack coming out of the generator building;

also of a little piece of sky. They brought me here later the day of the zapping. Alison fixed it all up. Lynx must have pointed his forelock straight at the Mayor.

At the beginning, they were just keeping an eye on me. I was allowed to walk around and take a shower. They also gave me Thorazine, to tone me down. Turned out, no way some new tranquilizer can beat out something as ancient as a suicide center that's been waiting to do its thing for practically forever.

Around a week after I made Alison hit me in the head, I was sitting there reading a book. Then, out of nowhere, I felt that I had to get rid of myself right away. Nothing like a voice inside of me giving me the order. It was more a unanimous decision of every part of my body to swap living for dying. At the same time, thinking perfectly clearly about implementing same in what seemed to be just a few seconds. Which shows how little time it takes to make arrangements for eternity. I checked out the possibilities in the room, one by one. No way of jumping out the window; it was shut tight. Besides, it was covered by the mesh I'd seen from the street. The look of those windows had always scared me when I walked past the Psycho a few times a day. Now that I was on the inside, it made sense to me. What self-respecting insane asylum would leave the windows open and uncovered?

No poison around; no plastic bag either, to wrap around my head. The best I could think of was the bed sheet. Made a beeline for it, rolled it up and tied one end around my neck. Then I looked around for a place where I could sling the other end. I kept feeling a peculiar rush, all the parts of my body on high alert, checking in at the same time. Hands tingling, heart racing. My gut squeezing away, like after a healthy dose of prunes. I was looking forward to an up-close and personal view of the *process* of dying; what happens during. The situation not the same as when you're ready to croak, and a couple of what they call "vital organs" get together and agree that enough is enough. It must be extra boring – when there's not even a remote possibility of the rest of you getting better – for your heart to have to beat on and on like some gone-crazy church bell, 24/24, 7/7. And how much interest can there be for the kidneys to keep on drip, drip, dripping? Having the two of them go – pretty soon, the brain gets in on the action too – you're liable not to notice the changeover between being in "critical condition" and being dead. Which is not my case at all, the whole combo of dying of "natural causes."

Now I would find out for myself what everybody who ever lived wondered about: the bottom line. Where does it all lead to? Right after your vital organs stop being so vital, do you wake up in what looks to you like the Borscht Belt, on a beautiful day in July? With your nearest and dearest waiting there to greet you at the bus stop in front of Grossinger's Hotel? Or is it goodbye Charlie, the moment expiration becomes your only inspiration, when all your being turns into nothingness? (Apologies to Sartre.) The latter has possibilities from the recycling viewpoint. Specifically: they take a filet of soul out of you, and transplant it into the next kid on the assembly line. That alternative doesn't hold a candle to the afterlife we keep trying to make reservations for. But, then again, who cares about your fundamentals going into somebody else, when you don't even know it's happening?

Just when things were getting interesting with the sheet, the nurse came in and stopped the whole show. It wasn't just any nurse, but the supervisor, Mr Nightingale, who put an end to what I was trying to do. Used to be in charge of the floor for the criminally insane. (Which terminology has always been a puzzle for me. Does it mean you're so insane that it's criminal? Or the other way around – you're so criminal, it's insane?) Those guys got farmed out to prison hospitals. So now, Mr Nightingale is in charge of the VIP floor where I'm a guest. Short, kind of dumpy-looking. Nice enough guy, but still, he's got these annoying tics. Probably comes from all the time he spent with the nutty baddies (or vice-versa). Doesn't walk straight into a room, sort of slides in along the wall.

Anyway, he made a big deal about me trying to hang myself. Took out a little whistle, and started blowing it like a super zealous football referee. Pretty soon, it was like Grand Central Station in there. Before I knew it, they had me spread-eagled on the bed, kept saying to me, "You don't want to do that, Dr Max…" Can't blame them, they didn't know my story, my privileged relationship with suicide. Alison was the only one in on that. As far as they were concerned, I was what's called a "suicide risk." Which entitled me to the whole package: regular visits from the psychiatrists, also from the suicide counselor. The job of the latter being to explore what's going on in your mind when you're planning it. Also, to talk you out of trying it again. In my case, same as a high school physics teacher going up against the atom scientists at Los Alamos.

Afterwards, they kept my door open at all times, with staff coming to check on me every few minutes. Changed the Thorazine to something else. No go – the new medicine didn't even make me sleepy. For sure, it didn't change my mind about what I wanted – needed – to do. The suicide center told this new drug to fuck off. Finally, they put a straitjacket on me, which kept me from using my arms. I found a way around that too, by banging my head against the side rails, hoping to get a bleed going inside. I must have made a lot of noise doing it, because they came running in right away and kept me from doing it again. All I ended up with was a monster headache. After that, no more honor system. I split my time between lying in bed (they padded the side rails) and sitting in a chair, with both arms and one leg tied down.

That's how close I came, playing chicken with the void. Maybe it was a good thing they didn't let me go through with it. Gave me a chance to think about what was happening, and how good it felt, that rush. I'd keep on trying until I got it right.

So what does a guy do when he's tied up, day and night? Somebody like me who's with it all the way? Nothing like the barely conscious crowd that collects bedsores like they're premium checks. The answer is, I watch TV a lot of the time. The remote control wedged in my right palm so I can change channels. Didn't take me long to get hooked on *The Horowitz Twins – Live!* A three times a week cable show, featuring Dr Melissa and Dr Samantha, who no way you can tell apart, except by their getups. Dr M wears blue scrubs, while Dr S sticks to the traditional greens. Both of them are gynecologists. According to the announcer, "they take time out of their busy schedules" for their favorite cause: "getting women in touch with their sexuality." Sound interesting? You bet your sweet ass. Especially if you're shackled down, 24/24.

They deal a lot with what you could call "societal issues." The first show I watched, the Gyn twins had this white-haired suit sitting between them. Introduced him as an expert in "Intimate Apparel Law." He had a prim look about him. To me, it looked like the only item of intimate apparel he ever got to see was his own jockey shorts. In a singsong voice, he droned on and on about a class action suit filed by the partners of ladies who were into pantyhose called "Trim and Comfy." Which is supposed to tighten up the tummy and the muscles you sit on, but – a tasteless way of putting it, I thought – "give where women are supposed to get." Anyway – a big manufacturing booboo. They made a whole batch that gave where they were supposed to tighten, and clamped down where they were supposed to give. Result? The ladies had multiple orgasms every day, meaning when they got home at night, all of them had symptoms of a serious case of been there, done that. No interest left in sex with their partners. The motive for the lawsuit.

People drop in to see me. Peter Bishop, the pathologist, and Louie Rosenkrantz, the guy who built the laser for me. Once in a while, even The Chief comes around. The way he behaves, that gives me a lot of hope. For my demise, I mean. When he gets – you could say almost human – with patients, it always means their end is near. That's the way he is with me.

Once or twice, even Persian Pete comes by. Rushes in in his scrub suit, the hair on his chest escaping every which way. Hoisting up his balls every couple of minutes, Italian style. A little rumble – like a drumstick playing a riff on a drum – emanating from there every time he does it. I'm sure it's Alison who makes him come to see me. He'll never know how close he came to getting zapped. Gives me the usual doctor bullshit: "You'll be fine Max. Just a matter of time!" He could show a little more interest, the ungrateful bastard. Was I right to give him a reprieve and take the hit myself? Too late now.

Of course, there's always Aunt Florence. During our weekly telephone talks, she kept bringing up the next summer, she knew a place where we could go away together, learn more German – with a French touch, ha-ha. Didn't tell her about my change of domicile. By this time, she'd reverted to her former aunt status for me. No use worrying her, telling her what I'd done and what I was hoping to do. But that French bit puzzled me, even if it was never going to happen. What in the world was she thinking of for an encore?

One day, Arlene I came to call. Didn't bother with flowers or candy. Brought me one of her old jeans, for sniffing purposes. Which they let me keep in my bed, like those security blankets babies get off on. Arlene II dropped by too. She'd married a rich guy, so no more denim trench coats for her. Sashayed in, covered in a queen-size mink. When she sat down, the coat opened up – nothing on underneath. Elena I also came to visit. Looking holy in her down-to-the-floor habit, big cross suspended from her neck. The nurses don't know what to make of this visiting Sister. Is she a relative or what? Otherwise, why would she plant a long kiss on my lips every time she comes and goes?

Marian is a regular, of course. Brings the mail; also some goodies from the Parthenon. A greasy hamburger, or even one of those bagels I used to love to hate. But the best thing about being a prisoner: I get to see Alison every day. She shows up after work, then spends a couple of hours sitting opposite me, her legs up on a little stool. Skirt like a wind tunnel. Underskirt Factor hitting me like a ton of bricks. Keeps telling me she knows for sure that the effects of the laser will start wearing off soon. So I can go back to being a regular citizen. Whatever that is.

That regular *tête-à-tête* is the high point of my days. If this was a movie, she'd be right about the need to kill myself gradually wearing off. Then I invent a new laser, which knocks my suicide center out for good: fight fire with fire. That's not all. The second laser just happens to work on the Penile Paradox too. Hits it square between the eyes. All of a sudden I get a full-time hard-on for Alison, and we walk out of the Psycho into the sunset, arm in arm.

But that isn't at all what I have in mind. I'd feel like a total schmuck if the need to kill myself ends up in a whimper. Hasn't happened yet, and I don't expect it to, either. All I know is, I am totally on board for what the center has to offer.

One day, Alison came in, all excited. They'd just established a Lectureship in my honor. Those are talks given by some visiting hotshot, giving the lowdown on his or her latest research. For that, they get a fee, plus a free trip, all expenses paid. In this case, to the Big Apple. Couldn't wait to find out who put up the money. Figured it had to be at least a $200,000 investment. Finally got around to asking. "Why, the Teitelbaums, of course," Alison answered. Being the object of a 24/7 suicide watch is not exactly the best way to climb the academic ladder, so I should have had a big inkling this was bound to happen. Namely, that I could kiss the Professorship I was supposed to get when I turned forty-five goodbye. The Chief must have had a word with them. "Poor Max," I could just hear him say, "The best way we can honor him, now that his eligibility for the Fido Professorship is out of the question, is to name a Lectureship after him." My bet is, he's taking the Fido Teitelbaum Professorship for himself.

Don't go around thinking it's all visits from old girlfriends, watching the Horowitz twins on TV, and Underskirt Factor appreciation. The burnt-out suicide center keeps sending me messages. Each time I get one, everything starts pulsating and tingling. Especially high-ticket items like the arms that open windows, and the legs that take the jump. Blood pouring into them, like floodwaters after two weeks of rain. Feels like they'd be extra light—while also packing a big wallop—if I was ever allowed to use them. Which I can't. And while my keepers have been hoping, expecting even, for me to get over my need to kill myself (as if it were the common cold,) I've been trying to come up with another plan. No way I'm going to lie around here, year after year, being kept alive so I won't make myself dead.

I was becoming pretty discouraged. But, one day, as I was looking at the little piece of sky they allow me, I saw a banner floating in front of me. Like the ones those little planes drag over Miami Beach, advertising McDonald's, or some local, bad-credit-OK used car dealer. Still, when I moved over a little bit, and I couldn't see the sky anymore, the banner was still there. Which suggested to me it was some kind of message. Looked like "VEGAS." Racked my brain for what that could mean. Russian Roulette? Then I got a better look. It was "VAGUS," not "VEGAS." It was a supreme revelation. Now I knew exactly what I had to do.

The vagus is a nerve which, when it's tickled, slows down the heart. It's deep in the body, but the beauty of it is you don't have to tickle it straight on. There's a way of making it work for you without even getting near it. If I could teach my vagus to make my heart beat slower and slower, I had a shot at getting to a point where there wouldn't be enough blood pumped to any of my organs. Nothing dramatic. For once, supply and demand going in the same direction.

No question that was the way to go. But how to do it? Two of the three ways to turn on the vagus didn't fit into my situation. That would require outside help. With both arms and one leg tied down, pressing on a certain spot in my neck, or giving the muscle of my anus a 7th-inning stretch were nonstarters. The only thing left for me: hold my breath and bear down, all at the same time. That's the Valsalva Maneuver, and it's guaranteed to slow the heart down to a walk. So I told my jailers I felt some skipped beats. That made them put me on a monitor. Between the monitor and the clock I could see from my bed, I'd be able to check how well

I was doing with the breath holding.

At first, every time I did the maneuver, not much change, just a few beats less. But after a while, if I gave a good squeeze without breathing, the monitor didn't like what it saw. A good sign. Didn't feel faint or anything—yet—but from my usual sixty or seventy, I was down to around fifty beats a minute. I had to learn how to hold my breath longer, train my body. The Valsalva Maneuver was starting to work, but it would take another few weeks for my breathing and my slowed-down heart to meet for a final rendezvous. At which point, when the rush and the tingling came over me, I'd be ready to do my bit. Hold my breath for a good long time and squeeze down like there's no tomorrow. Which there won't be.

Now that I know how I'm going to do it, I feel more hopeful.. Before, I had a lot of guilt about not coming through for my suicide center. Now it's just a matter of time, while I'm patiently waiting on my own, personal Death Row.

Do I have any regrets about wanting to knock myself off? I mean, am I 100% on board all the time about wanting to knock myself off? The answer is, I'd have to be crazy not to once in a while question what I had Alison do to me. But what made me fool her into shooting the laser at my locus ceruleus was a combination of scientific curiosity and disappointment in love. The opposite—scientific disappointment and curiosity in love—would have put a whole different slant on things. I wouldn't be lying here now all tied up, getting my jollies from the likes of the Horowitz twins' take on defective pantyhose. But there's no use moaning and groaning, or asking "do we really have to go through with this?" No way the suicide center is going to let me off the hook.

CHAPTER ELEVEN

ALISON BEARING GIFTS

Mid-December, 1984

Something really weird happened one night, around 1am. The reason I know is that there is a big clock on the wall, facing my bed. I even remember what was playing on the radio: Mozart's *Don Giovanni*. The hotshot who fucks all the women and slices up most of the men, while singing his ass off the entire time. My kind of guy. I was just getting myself into it, when, out of nowhere, the radio goes dead, and the lights in the hall go out. The shades in my room were drawn, so not even a glimmer coming from the direction of the windows. I hear these footsteps coming into my room. I ask who's there – no answer. I'm tied down, so nothing I can do about finding out. Pretty soon, I feel a tug on the cord holding up my pajama bottoms. Right after, there's this gentle pulling, to the point where the top of the bottoms meets the bottom of my bottom. What's this? They're taking rectal temperatures now, in the middle of the night? Except, I'm not getting turned over on my side. Instead, I'm feeling this warm, smooth hand, stroking the inside of my thighs. First one, then the other, back and forth like that. A maneuver guaranteed to make the ball on the side that's getting stroked go up and down like a yo-yo. That's the cremasteric reflex, a well-known time and motion saver for hookers. While the testicles are doing their dance, in all the excitement, the one who's getting stroked gets a big hard-on.

Right off the bat, I began to have misgivings. As you must realize by now, I'm a pretty conservative person. To entrust my blossoming hard-on to somebody I can't see, who hasn't said a word, where I don't even know if it's a woman (or God forbid a man), that made me pretty nervous. Just as I was going to give out with a big *Oy Vey* (trans: SOS), this other smooth hand gets clapped over my mouth, while the first one is still stroking my thighs. What now wrapped itself around my hard-on, was something located halfway between the two hands – a mouth.

Ever hear about the zipless fuck? It goes on in the dark, with somebody you never met before, in a train going through a super-long tunnel. The activity I was being subjected to was not exactly the same. I was lying there trussed up like a chicken ready for the rotisserie, with about as much choice as the former about who was going to do what to me. But the anonymous part was a lot like it. Still, a zipless fuck is way better than a fuckless zip. That's all that was available to guys like me, growing up in the Fifties. Got help taking my penis out of its holding pen. So far, so good. But after that, lots of rubbing, mainly with handkerchiefs. Or, if you got lucky, with pinched together thighs or pushed towards each other rolls of tummy baby fat. Or, on your birthday, being allowed to do the same, but this time with your penis as the centerpiece between budding breasts enjoying a brief furlough from their training bra.

Still, what hit me most was the odor. That combo of foot lotion and expensive shoe leather, mixed in with maybe a couple of drops of inter-toe sweat. What I'd smelled about Alison since that first time we'd walked down from Lynx's office. No Underskirt Factor evident. At this point – if it really was Alison – she would have been standing, not sitting. Therefore, no wind tunnel effect. Still, no question it was who I thought it was. Once she got going, I could sense her nodding away for all she was worth. Same as what I saw her doing to Persian Pete, that night in his apartment.

Here was this woman who I had a major case of the hots for, ever since we met. With the Penile Paradox chugging away all along. Now I'm in restraints. Can't move, except if you count my left leg. How much more at a disadvantage could I be? That would make my potency potential with somebody who had a 99% probability of being Alison even worse than when I was a free man and subject to the Paradox. But what actually happened was the complete opposite. Got this major hard-on as soon as the likely Alison put her hands on me. When that forward tilt of her head was dedicated 100% to me.

She applied her talents here the same way she got her Princeton PhD. Mature judgment, creativity, constructive use of the literature, and, goes without saying, oral skills. She has it all. Of course, I wondered why my Penile Paradox took the night off when it faced its biggest ever challenge. Could it be the Paradox malfunctions in deep darkness? Or does an active suicide center, in some way, interfere with the Paradox? I'm not likely to come up with an answer during my (shortened) lifetime. Main thing is, she went to all this trouble – in the middle of the night yet – to make me feel good. Same as throwing a surprise party for your nearest and dearest. That's when I decided to go out on this particular high. No way I was going to let that unique experience with Alison be anything but my last one. Ever.

Jews don't go in for extreme unction. Somehow, getting oil dripped on you when you're too sick to fight back is not for us. But what about extreme junction? Sometime in the next few days,

I had to let the message the suicide center sent me like clockwork, hook up with the Valsalva. Went into high gear with the breathing training after that. Pretty soon, I could hold my breath long enough to get my heart down to around forty beats a minute. The numbers not even close to making me conk out, but getting there. No way is this going to be one of those long Jewish goodbyes. The kind where you put your coat on, but forget to leave; just keep yakking away.

Never talked to Alison about what happened that night. If I'd thanked her, she would have denied it. Plus maybe laugh in my face, give me one of those haughty *shikse* turnoffs: "The very thought of it makes me want to barf!" Better not say anything.

CHAPTER TWELVE

EVERY TIME WE SAY
GOODBYE, I DIE A LITTLE

Late December, 1984

A last go-around with things you take for granted; until it hits you that pretty soon you're never going to see them again. My left large toe, for instance. Always favored it over the right, seeing as it has this little tuft of hair growing out of it. Also, the knob growing out of my right wrist, the one I fell on as a kid.

My penis I never took for granted. I have to make my goodbyes there too. To those of you who own one, I don't have to tell you how preoccupied you can get with it. Men are always zeroing in on where it's been, where it is at any given moment, and where it's wandering to next. Tied up like I was, I didn't have much of a chance to commune with it. Sort of lost touch. Still, I'm sad this is the end of our relationship. We've been through so much together.

And then there are the objects – they call them "inanimate," but to me they have an identity all their own. My stainless steel urinal for instance, the one with the little yellow dents in it, that's always ready for me at the side of my bed. Also, the electric clock on the wall, and the rocking chair Alison sits in, from which she sends off her Underskirt Factor. And the smokestack I can see through my window, always puffing out a white vapor, like they're electing a new Pope every day of the week.

Not to speak of the Horowitz twins. Tuned in to their program for what was bound to be the last time. It couldn't have been a better sendoff. Featured a lipstick for those "other lips." They had the inventor of a gadget called "Labistik," Elle Majora was her name, as a guest on the program. It looked like a regular lipstick—just a lot longer—with a little mirror like the one dentists use coming out of one side. Inventors are always out to find things they want the public to think they need. Ms Majora summed it up. "So the lap-dancer hidden away in every woman has a chance to come out." Big ovation and stamping of feet from the studio audience. I don't have any personal experience with that kind of cosmetics; at least as far as I know. Whenever I plunge under the blankets in the dark, I never come back to the surface with smudged lipstick on my face.

The Horowitz twins don't endorse products on their show. That's how they keep their scientific integrity. But the one in blue—Dr Melissa—was starting to get that look in her eye; like where's the nearest Labistik franchise? Dr Samantha was staying neutral. Put on the puss she must use to announce to somebody they're going to have septuplets—dead serious, no crapping around. If the viewers couldn't make up their minds, her look suggested, why not talk it over with their clergywoman or their vaginal esthetics advisor? Whatever—I feel sad about never keeping company with the Horowitz twins again.

I'm up to a minute at a time of no breathing, together with pushing down at the same time, which brings my pulse down to the high thirties. Giving me a feeling like my head got unscrewed from my neck. All of which means, the next time the suicide center sends out its message, the rest of me will be ready, willing and able to deliver the goods.

Sure enough, early this morning, I'd just turned the radio on. For what is going to happen very soon, the music was appropriate. "The Stars and Stripes Forever," played by the Marine Corps, Army, and Navy bands. For some reason, the Air Force band had flown the coop. Anyway, that's when I felt that rush again, every part of my body on alert, like it was waiting for something to happen. My ears ringing and my scalp itching, like I ran out of anti-dandruff shampoo. Too much going on for me to do a last-minute check on if I was really going to go through with this. Went right to the breath-holding and the Valsalva. All that training was paying off. After a couple of minutes, the monitor and the clock told me my pulse was down to the low thirties. That's when I started to feel *schwarz far die oigen* (trans: ready to keel over.) But, since I'm lying down in bed, the blood keeps coming to my head. Meaning I still know what's going on; at least for a little while yet. So I can find out what dying is really like.

I'm pushing down hard, taking a breath here and there. No revelations yet. I'm starting to feel kind of warm and fuzzy, like those explorers when they're ready to freeze to death. Can't see the clock or monitor anymore, but estimate my heart rate is about twenty-five. Waiting for something to happen. Meanwhile, all these thoughts keep horning in. Not the kind that are up to the level of the occasion.

What I keep thinking about is banal stuff, considering the seriousness of the occasion. Like the logistics of my funeral. They're bound to do it at the Fred Cummings Funeral Chapel, on Madison and 75th. Nice limestone building. A specialist doorman out front, "Mourner Greeter" imprinted on the front of his top hat. Around the corner, on a side street, the takeaway entrance (and exit) for the mourned. In the old days, Riverview Chapel, on Amsterdam in the West 70s, was where anybody Jewish who was somebody, went when they went. In more recent times, people of the Hebrew persuasion – the way we're treated, believe me, we need to be persuaded – get a 48-hour guest membership at Cummings. Only two requirements: you have to have an up-to-date death certificate, and somebody – in my case, the Department – has to be flush enough to come up with the funds. Still, I wouldn't recommend they bury the Lubavitcher Rebbe from there. I mean, hundreds of recruits from Yeshiva boot camps swarming all over Madison Avenue, tearing at their clothes. Bouncing up and down, pounding their chests, while they're waiting to hand-carry the coffin across the Triborough Bridge to Beth Deth, the Chasidic cemetery off the Long Island Expressway. Almost as bad as Puerto Rican Day, when the eponymous insist on barbecuing on the steps of the Metropolitan Museum. What I'm trying to say is, being laid out at Cummings is more for "moderate Jews." No throwing yourself in front of the coffin, making them roll it over you to get it out the door. Above all, no wailing or screaming. Although a medium loud *geschrei,* a mix of sobbing and *kvetching* about the untimely removal of the mourned, is permitted.

Also, will The Chief cancel the operating schedule so they can have the funeral on a weekday? Or will they keep me on the rocks until Sunday, so they can sandwich the obsequies in between *The Times* early in the morning, and the football game in the afternoon?

And don't forget the dress code. For sure, yarmulkes all over the place; The Chief, and the whole Department wearing them. With neurosurgeons, seems to me "skullcap" is a more appropriate term. Jews wear theirs in a kind of throwaway style. Casual, slipping this way or that; no big deal. But put them on Gentiles for funerals, weddings, whatever, then it's a whole other story. Once they put them on, they're afraid to take them off. Don't want to do the wrong thing. While Jews, most of the time, can't wait to get rid of them. Ends up a big mishmash, with the Gentiles looking devout, and the Jews looking like Gentiles.

Also, there's the fledglings. Wouldn't it be appropriate for them to wear black scrub suits when they pay their last respects to the guy who kept them out of trouble, day in, day out? Like sporting a black armband.

And here's my biggest concern: how is it going to be with Alison? Will she just be dabbing at her eyes, all the time stealing looks at her watch? Figuring she'd done her bit with the anonymous blowjob, now we were even?

It's a fact: plenty of people (including myself) fret over how their funerals reflect on their popularity. Either their prestige has always been on the high side, so what happens at their funeral is just more of the same. Or they were always in a low self-esteem category, and this is their very last chance to shine. (Rising being out of the question by now.) You don't even have to be dying, to wonder how many are going to make how much of a *geschrei* when you kick the bucket. For most people, it's a lifelong worry.

Meanwhile, there's something else on my mind: my grave. It's not what kind of a stone they're going to pick, or what's going to be chiseled on it. None of that stuff; I couldn't care less. But what does upset me, is what I'm just starting to remember now. The ground rules laid out in a fancy document, the Protocols of the Elders of Mt Zion. Something in it about suicides having to be buried outside the cemetery walls; no exceptions. That was all well and good in the old days, when graveyards sat in the middle of the countryside. But Mt Zion Cemetery happens to be chocka-block with Route 22, in New Jersey, one of the busiest commuter arteries. Strictly speaking, it's an artery in the mornings, when it feeds New York City, and a vein in the evenings, when it drains it. If you get buried outside the walls, it's got to be under Route 22. Traffic jams, with people throwing their cold McNuggets right on top of my remains. Followed by chasers of cold coffee poured out of those Styrofoam cups.

Now I'm down to fifteen beats a minute, give or take a couple. The warm and fuzzy is just plain fuzzy by now. I'm starting to think it may be a *mitzvah* (trans: a good deed that's not tax deductible) for people to die, not knowing what's going on. Because for me – at least so far – the experience has been miserable. I mean, pedestrian thoughts superimposed on feeling more and more like shit.

And still, these practical concerns. All of a sudden, I'm thinking of the books I'm leaving behind. My clothes, I couldn't care less about. Anybody who wants my chinos and hushpuppies, plus a few shirts and sweaters, is welcome to them. But my books, I feel like I'm abandoning them. That I thought only of myself when I got that laser shot at me. What's going to become of them now? It's as if you have pets at home. A couple of dogs, a few cats, and maybe a bird or a goldfish. With the space situation in Manhattan being what it is, who's going to take them in when you die? Nobody I know has extra room for a couple of thousand books. Besides, it's like your dog bites, and the bird is always getting pneumonia. My books aren't exactly what you'd call "mainstream." They're not the kind you can spend your evenings curled up on the sofa with. I can just see them being dumped on the street, nobody there to rescue them, waiting for the garbage truck. But some of them could even be bound for a worse fate. Ripped off in the middle of the night by some homeless guy, and assigned to latrine duty. All I can say is, the whole thing makes me very sad. I wish Alison was here right now, so she could at least plant a kiss on me before I die.

By now, I'm really bummed. Went to all this trouble, and I don't know one bit more about this dying business than before I started. I'd have liked at least a hint that something good is going to happen afterwards. A little wink, maybe a friendly voice that says "*Bubbele*, it's OK. Be a little patient, and you'll see how great the afterlife can be." But nothing, nothing at all? Is this worth getting myself knocked off for?

Makes me seriously wonder if I should have fooled with Mother Nature. Go do hocus-pocus with the only game in town, namely living. You end up like me. No girl, no life, no Fido Teitelbaum Professorship. Just a no-sense-of-humor Valsalva Maneuver that's about to do me in any minute.

Can't drag this out much longer. My heart is beating so slow, it feels like it's just trembling. Now I'm seeing that banner again. "The Song is Over, But the Melody Lingers On" is what it says. Sending me a hopeful message, with maybe positive possibilities for the future. To which I'm going to squeeze out my last words ever:

It should only be…

THE END

Acknowledgments

Kisses to my grandchildren, Nico and Allia, for the intense interest they have shown in their Opi's writing. My thanks to my sons Paul and John and my daughter-in-law, Yasmin Hai, for critical readings of the manuscript and ever helpful suggestions. I am thankful to my daughter-in-law, Michèle Blair, for her encouragement and support. Tariq Goddard believed in this book from the beginning, and his benevolent critique nudged me into doing my best to justify his judgment. For that, I am deeply grateful. Thanks to Josh Turner, who was responsible for the coherent copy editing and beyond. Kudos to Johnny Bull, for his inspired cover. Thanks also to Lucy Ellmann. My gratitude to my stepson Mark Brewin and his wife Georgette, who first put me on the trail of Tariq Goddard. My loving appreciation to my wife Helen for reading and listening to various versions of this work over the past years. She has helped even more than she knows.

Repeater Books

is dedicated to the creation of a new reality. The landscape of twenty-first-century arts and letters is faded and inert, riven by fashionable cynicism, egotistical self-reference and a nostalgia for the recent past. Repeater intends to add its voice to those movements that wish to enter history and assert control over its currents, gathering together scattered and isolated voices with those who have already called for an escape from Capitalist Realism. Our desire is to publish in every sphere and genre, combining vigorous dissent and a pragmatic willingness to succeed where messianic abstraction and quiescent co-option have stalled: abstention is not an option: we are alive and we don't agree.